The Terrors of Dr Treviles

The Peter Redgrove Library

Other Peter Redgrove books available from Stride:

The Peter Redgrove Library:
1. *In the Country of the Skin*
2. *The Terrors of Dr. Treviles**
3. *The Glass Cottage**
4. *The God of Glass*
5. *The Sleep of the Great Hypnotist*
6. *The Beekeepers*
7. *The Facilitators*
8. *The Colour of Radio: Essays and Interviews*
[*with Penelope Shuttle]

The Laborators
Abyssophone
Orchard End
What the Black Mirror Saw
Sheen
A Singer for the Silver Goddess

A Curious Architecture [contributor]
Earth Ascending [contributor]

i.m. Peter Redgrove:
Full of Star's Dreaming: Peter Redgrove 1932-2003

The Terrors of Dr Treviles

A Romance

Peter Redgrove

with Penelope Shuttle

The Terrors of Dr Treviles
This edition 2006

ISBN 1-905024-09-6

Cover design by Neil Annat
Cover photos © Alistair Fitchett
Used with kind permission of the artist

The Peter Redgrove Library
is published by
Stride Publications
4b Tremayne Close
Devoran
Cornwall TR3 6QE
England

www.stridebooks.co.uk

Thanks

The Peter Redgrove Library is grateful to the following subscribers who have helped make the publication of these titles possible:

Cliff Ashcroft
Andrew Bailey
Martin Bax
Hazel Carruthers
Philip Fried
Mark Goodwin & Nikki Clayton
David Grubb
Michael Longley
Adrian & Celia Mitchell
Brian Louis Pearce
Malcolm Ritchie
Geoff Sutton & Bernard Gilhooly
Leonie Whitton & David Westby

to the following for help, encouragement and support in other ways:

Tony Frazer
Neil Roberts
Penelope Shuttle
the late Philip Hobsbaum

and to Arts Council England, South West for financial support.

Introduction

Written in conjunction with Penelope Shuttle, this second novel of Peter Redgrove's first appeared in 1974. It demonstrates the power of that imagination with which its protagonists and authors are concerned and is distinguished throughout by its invention, sweep, vitality of spirit, harnessed through ordeal. It vibrates with authorial energy and lets us into the *feel* of a setting or incident as though unlocking a secret gate. Yet its most endearing feature is arguably the way it is bubbling and running over with the presence of its authors, as though they are both beside us as we read. This is not to say that Redgrove is in all particulars or any to be identified with Dr. Gregory Treviles' amalgam of a scientific don with the giant at Cerne Abbas, or Shuttle with the characters of Robyn and her mother or Brid. But hers are the poems at the end of the book that in 'Travelling' or 'A Twelvemonth', for example, reveal her gift for moth's-wing detail and velvet phrase.

From the same period comes *The Hermaphrodite Album*, their joint work of poetry, in which it can be difficult to discern who wrote what. Both books are celebrations; both suggest their sheer enjoyment in setting about their mutual task. Yet in *The Terrors of Dr Treviles*, despite the grim, frightening or fantastic elements its theme demands, the sense of them sharing with us the *fun* they are having together in the process of its composition is particularly evident. Take the amusing list of books in Part One (section 11) ranging from *Gray's Anatomy* to *Voodoo Queen, You Only Live Twice, a Guide to Tintagel*. Take the reference to Gregory reading Redgrove's own book *The Force* (1966) in the train (Part One, section 23). The fact is that Gregory is actually putting it down and that — to confuse the issue further — that book is dedicated to Dr. E.C. Gregory, founder of the Fellowship at Leeds University which Redgrove held from 1962 to 1965. Take the disarmingly quaint farewell, 'The End of our Book', at the close of the Robyn poems. It is not always fun without moment. The poetry reading and wryly earnest discussion in Part Two (section 14) is not only all too plausible — and risible; it features a poem by Redgrove himself in memory of his brother. But there is a like engagement in the description of the simplest incident or setting. A typical case is the closing paragraph of Part One. Its short sentences and charged verbs enable us to live the experience, as the parties 'went through . . . looked . . . pointed . . . came puffing' (the train at this point acts almost as a character) '. . . slid past them . . . looked through . . . made a quick gesture . . . a door opened . . . down stepped . . . glances swept but did not meet . . . as Robyn pushed her way into the train.'

Quest is the theme, the search for the self or another's self — or that self's underside — and a finding. It primarily concerns Gregory here, though his stepdaughter Robyn's relationship with him, which interplays with her mother Mamie's influence, and with Robyn helping Brid to find *her* self, are important components. The masks which finally slip from Gregory's face at the book's close recall Wilde's *The Picture of Dorian Gray* up to a point. But in the case of Treviles, as all 'his terrors pass by him in vision' he is released. 'His own face greets him in the mirror.' One is left thinking of Redgrove's quote from Hesse's *Steppenwolf* in his *The Force* which Gregory was reading:

> 'Man . . . is an experiment and a transition. He is nothing else than the narrow and perilous bridge between nature and spirit. His innermost destiny drives him on to the spirit and to God. His innermost longing draws him back to nature, the mother. Between these two forces his life hangs tremulous and irresolute.'

The structure of the book appealingly echoes the patterns of drama and music, with its three acts or movements; Robyn's *Candle Poems* as a kind of Curtain-Piece or Coda, and Part Three corresponding to a Shakespearian last Act.

Like any artefact the book has its affinities even if, like a stack on the Cornish Coast, it stands separately from them. Alan M. Kent's *The Literature of Cornwall* offers insight into other Cornish-set fiction while links with Hesse and Wilde have been noted. Its subtitle *A Romance* recalls John Cowper Powys and there is kinship not only with the scope and zest of *A Glastonbury Romance* (albeit in fewer words) but with the kind of characters we find in (say) *Weymouth Sands*. A case can also be made for

A.S. Byatt's later *Possession* and *Angels and Insects* being distantly related. Take the mix of darker elements with light, the sensuous with the intellectual, the quest, the poems, the narrative strata, the tour through the complex, riskier aspects of the self and its relationships, though Byatt clearly is the more mainstream writer.

But this is its authors' book and no one else's. It is vital still with their insight and movement. It illustrates both a high point in their creativity and their pleasure in each other.

Brian Louis Pearce

Se tu avessi cento larve sopra la faccia, non mi sanen chiuse le tue cogitazion, quantunque parve.

If thou hadst a hundred masks on thy face, I would know thy smallest thought.

Purgatorio: Canto XV, 127-9

e come l'aere, quand' è ben piorno, per l'altrui raggio che in sè si riflette di diversi color diventa adorno . . .

and as the air from outer rays reflected within, glows with rainbow colour when charged with rain . . .

Purgatorio: Canto XXV, 91-3

Who, then, evolved the sea-blooms from the clouds
Diffusing balm in that Pacific calm?
C'était mon enfant, mon bijou, mon âme.

Wallace Stevens: *Sea Surface Full of Clouds*

Part One

Robyn to Gregory

I

There are three pulses, and a trough. All day, her thumbs have been on backwards. This wave will not break. She wishes to break into the trough. As the cavern grows greater, the head bends straining, wishing to break. The neck and shoulders which should be green and cool, streak with white pains. The head contemplates that cavern, where the current reverses.

All day, her thumbs have been on backwards. She has lost her great toes, and her feet tumble. She has barked her shin on the corner of sharp slate under the mattress, and she cut her hand on one of the old wineglasses as she picked it out of the dish-water with her backwards-reaching thumb. The globes of blood swelled like black balloons on the breadboard, making it like a butcher's block of headsman's wood. Its notches of everyday use were hacked blows. The blood tasted salt and rich. She got a plaster out of the bathroom and bound it up.

Gregory was away at a psychological conference. He was never absent at this time of the month if he could help it, since he maintained that she was prophetic in the instant before the blood flowed, and in the instant that it stopped. During her period — once it had begun, that is — she always dreamed vividly. Last month she had been at a festival in her dreams and was courted by a magnificently-muscled centaur. He was grizzled, his face fully human, and he carried a great goblet of red wine in which small flowers were floating. He gently took her by the shoulder and made her sip this wine. Then she was on his back, her hands clasped across his chest, and they were speeding across a desert towards a mountain. Once she looked behind her, and her shriek awoke her. The sea was at their heels in a tidal flood taller than them both, centaur and rider.

Gregory liked her to fantasise on her dreams. Or he would. They'd lie together in the mornings and continue the dreams like a morning bedtime story. Gregory was something of a specialist at this — he was a dream-therapist and the technique was called 'active imagination'. After the conference — which was a kind of ecumenical meeting between psychologists and churchmen — he said that he would go into retreat, it was time for him to take stock of his own interior life. One year in four, he believed, it was vital for any professional man to do this.

As for Robyn, she liked the opposite technique. Gregory loved to bring the dream into waking life. She loved to use objects and actions of waking life to bring herself closer to the dream. She loved magic.

It was her time then for a little practical magic. Red-haired as a lithium flame, white and slim as a candle, she would burn candles, and she would bring the darkened moon down into her house.

2

The silhouette of a man at a table glowing in the last sunshafts, studiously reading a letter, finger to brow. An anonymous letter. A woman pinning nappies up in the back garden. Her man must be out at the pub, she is washing nappies instead of preparing the supper. Hens that do not scare as the train rides above them on its embankment. The flash of sunvivid laburnum in a darkening garden. Surely they do not bloom now the nights are drawing in? Frosted windows in dirty brick. Through a tilted pane row upon row of workers bent over miniature lathes. The tea-trolley passes between them. It is a missile factory.

Images from the train journey flicker through Treviles's bent head as he admits to himself that the eminent speaker is not yet interesting. He lifts his head and looks round the room that is equipped with a giant's staircase rising towards nothing at all — an amphitheatre like Cornish Gwennap Pit where Wesley preached — on which are arranged benches and writing desks. The lecture-room is only half-full: there are a hundred delegates listening to the lecture, which is on 'Orthomolecular Psychiatry'. Gregory notices that no delegate is looking directly at the lecturer. He steals a glance himself. Endenberg, the leading authority in his field, is a big, shapeless man with a very clear voice. Now he is delivering astonishing news. It is a case-history of a man who suffered constant hallucinations of the 'openings into the other world' variety — like the Magritte painting, his fireplace would without warning become the tunnel for a tiny steam train that as soon as it had got past the hearth filled the room with the cinematograph flicker of sequent windows and the ringing clangour of rolling stock. Afterwards, he would be blind and deaf for a while, in great distress from the noise, and blind, he said, from the steam that filled the room.

Endenberg was saying that they fed this patient with five grams of vitamin C and one gram of the love-vitamin, E, each day for a week. At the end of the week, this patient who had suffered the train for perhaps ten times a day for ten years, much emaciated from lack of sleep and interruption of meals, was eating and sleeping normally. The only remaining fragment of his trouble was the dream that he had always before he woke up — that he stepped into a train that carried him towards the daylight.

Treviles made a note about this on the pad in front of him. Then he looked round again. Still nobody watched the lecturer as he spoke. Several of the clergymen were writing — he knew that many of them were also doctors. Others, like his friend Bodkin — not present at this session — were merely enthusiasts.

Now Endenberg began to recall the work of John White, who had proved in the 1960s that voice could affect molecular structure. White caused a dozen very warty-skinned subjects to be hypnotised, and in deep trance they were told that the warts on the right hand sides of their bodies would disappear, but not those on the left. It was so. White repeated these experiments with allergic subjects sensitised to a simple protein. He told the allergy to go, the weeping spots, the blotches, and they went. The simplest hypothesis was that the molecular structure had changed. And that every time we heard a voice from the outside, every time some person told us a lie, or a fact, the grain of our reality, the molecular structure of our body changed accordingly. The flicker of TV produced a light trance, the bad news of the telecasts produced bad changes, the bodies sneezed them out — and behold a 'flu epidemic. The depressions, the lurches of mood in 'flu — these were the voices of the mutated proteins, they spoke of bad news because they were thus spoken to, talking back to life in its own language. As he said this Endenberg sneezed suddenly, and still speaking, pulled the clean white handkerchief from his top pocket and wiped his nose and mouth with it. Treviles found himself stifling a sneeze, and took out his handkerchief. As he did so he saw out of the corner of his eye the flutter of white as the delegates all wiped their noses, still not looking at each other or the lecturer. Gregory laughed suddenly, loudly. The hundred-headed lecture audience turned in one swift reflex and was aware of him. He faced two hundred eyes. He got to his feet. The lecturer said, 'and with that, I have no more to say'. Treviles, still on his feet, began applauding. Immediately, two hundred hands began applauding. Endenberg bowed slightly at Gregory Treviles, and sat down.

3

A candle increases the size of a room. The day before yesterday she lit the black candle there that can burn for a week. Now she stands motionless in front of the wooden door of the small stone room that is the oldest part of the house. She has already closed the door of the narrow hallway so that the passage is isolated, like an air-lock. She finds that her fingers are trembling. With her trembling fingers she turns off the electric light in this hallway, her light-lock. Her eyes at first tell her that she is sunk in abyssal black, standing in the middle of a lump of asphalt, a lump of coal, a pool of mud, baked into a brick, standing in a flue choked with soot, inside a winter tree. Then the sensations of suffocation are replaced by the sense of a new space, great enlargement. Her blinded eyes are awakening her other senses. A draft that plays about her ankles brings touch-patterns of the things it has touched, as a pebbled stream swirls among its pebbles; she feels its flowing grain. The light switch is the smooth head of an idol, and a minute chip out of the ebonite shapes itself to a face under her fingertips. Her sense of smell is animal-acute; it is as if louvres have opened in her blind face. The little stream of air that enters the dark carries much information: she smells the hot metal of the electric fire in the outer room, the books read aloud in slow seepage of paper, glue and ink; perhaps that is the odour of gossamer and the heavy cashew smell of a spider behind the electric clock.

She realises that in this reverie of her under-used senses, she has nevertheless been seeing clearly for some time. There is a gap under the door and through that gap comes a steady faint glow that is both bright and gentle at once. The room is candle-lit in her absence. The candle-stick on the bare table, the empty room, the empty chairs, the carpet untrodden, the pictures unlooked at, the shelf of books unopened. The candle is at work in this closed room. Its flame traces out with the room's air two great implicit wings or warm hemispheres, pulling the dusty air through itself and thrusting it up to the ceiling where it fountains down again to the flame. Robyn wishes she could devise a way of entering this room without disturbing these two great candle-air hemispheres in the gentle brilliant light. Surely the twenty-four hours since she left the room untended to enable the candle to round its patterns are long enough for it to find a perfect equilibrium? Could she not slip in somehow through the layers and sit in her chair in front of the candle like the expected thought of a calm mind, rather than a nightmare visitor bringing gales and a new pattern? At any rate she will enter as softly as she can.

4

He called himself a psychotherapist, but truly, he wondered if his year off were not rather overdue! Not a single one of his colleagues had been persuaded to admit to the simultaneous and identical gesture of nose-wiping that Gregory had observed in the lecture-theatre. The lecturer, Endenberg, had left for Prague, and there had been no chance to speak to him. Treviles found himself mentally predicting what each of the psychologists would say about his observation — to a man the clergymen would guffaw as if he were joking. The Reichian — why were Reichians always men? wondered Gregory — would say that he had been overtaken by a sudden inner vision of the white flash of his spunk; the Freudian, Exler, would maintain that the event was a recollective fantasy of infantile masturbation, and that the handkerchiefs (seen white because the Censor laundered the true texture and the true filthiness of guilt out of the fabric) were the collective ghost of his holding blanket; the Kleinian, a slim sensible woman unaccustomed to talking to grown-ups, since her practice was chiefly among people under ten years old, would speak of the contemplative white screen of suckling on which his babyhood projected fantasies and would point out that it was the *breast* pocket that provided the handkerchief; the Adlerian, a shabby doctor with a sadly diminished practice, would speak of a fantasy of superiority and the control by hypnosis of a round century of his fellow-men; and the Jungian would tell of the alchemical albedo, the great and pervasive whiteness, and warn him of a sudden depression, nigredo. So he asked the Jungian. She replied, looking at him steadily, 'Yes, I saw that. I didn't believe it either. I'm very glad you told me. We were all listening much more closely than we realised. I've heard that Crowley could, in a street, walk so precisely like the man he was following that when the follower tripped and missed his step deliberately, the followed would stumble. Did you hear that Endenberg uses occult methods in his practice?' 'So do I', said Gregory, 'in a sense. I like to play with the dream and return it to the dreamer so that he can dream more of it. This is frowned upon, I expect you frown upon it, but it's as the Rabbis used to say: "The Dream follows the Interpretation".' 'I think this means that we are all sleeping children who are geniuses, Dr Treviles.' 'Yes, I believe this. Like children, our unknown abilities must play.' 'Don't you think this is destructive? I can't afford to take risks. I'm in practice for my living! No, I'm not angry. I'm a good ambulance-woman, that's all. I wish I were more. I've no time to study,' said Brid Hare, sharply, 'anyway,' as Treviles was about to speak, 'I'm not sure I want to study with a man analyst. Not after the last time.' 'Are you going to Evensong in the Abbey?' 'No, I want to see the old films.' 'May I take you there? We could have a drink beforehand. Maybe take a bottle in.' 'Please yourself, Gregory. I've got other fish to fry.'

I'd rather have the interpretations from Reichian, Freudian and the rest, thought Gregory, than that fully-fashioned bitch. I'll drink with Bodkin, that priestly schoolchild. You can't call him heavy. He'd sink, and he loves skating over deep waters. He'll know all about Endenberg, from the outside.

5

As Robyn opened the door, it was like launching a boat. It was like willows trailing in the water, like a distant flock of birds turning an acre's mask to her that swept off like a snatched-away tablecloth. It was like the glimpse of a river plunging into a tunnel, it was like winds through the forest, it was like opening an underground chamber, it was like opening a room under the sea. Sometimes when one enters a room it seems that the people in it have been standing quite still and only began moving with a frightening and unnatural vivacity the moment your foot crossed the threshold. Robyn knew that this was true of the shadows in the room that had been standing still and streaming upwards in the closed room for a day and a night, and it was her entrance that started them moving like a crowd hurrying from an underground station, like a crowd running from an airshow disaster, like a crowd of priests running from the horsed conquerers, like an entire forest felled at one blow, like the Houses of Parliament executed with one axe. As the door opened the candle-flame, like a bright eye looking sideways at her from a pillow, bent so hard that it seemed to wink, and then streamed upwards trembling with light that was almost dazzling. In the room furnished with a plain solid table and gate-back chairs it was like a foot in an ants' nest, like monkeys and spiders fighting in a cage, like the tumbling of many express trains filled with people into chasms of darkness that exploded with light and went dark. Gently she closed the door and it was like standing in a webwork of nerve cells twinkling with messages, for a moment like standing in a foam of black and white bubbles that hurried upwards, a foamy sea of white and black into which she was plunging. Her skin felt a sudden excitement like an interesting sexual suggestion, as though Gregory had taken out a whip and then kissed her navel, kissed her ear. It was like standing inside a clock hiding from the sunshine, it was like entering an old clock whose mainspring was a lighted black candle, and whose escapement was the rhythm of stray winds. An aeolian clock.

Moving as gently as possible she sits down at the table in front of the candle. The room is neither cold nor warm. She trimmed the wick before she left yesterday, and there is no pungency from the candle, but in the air which, from having passed through the living flame again and again before entering her lungs, is crackling and vibrant like flame, there is also the smell of wax that is warm, like the faint smell that clings to the skins of very young babies.

She settles her body in the chair so that her spine is straight, and allows it to relax so that her flesh hangs passive from her ribs. Gradually the wave gathers in her neck but something about the silence, something about the candle-air allows it to pass freely there and through her head but instead of making her feel that her head is about to drop into her lap with its weight, snapping her neck like a dry twisted bough as it does so, the crest of the wave passes into the feeling of her hair which looks black and not red in the candlelight, passes out of the crown of her head and runs over her body in a flowing which is like the melting of a rigid habit in a lover's bed. Her hands feel naturally left and right on her knees, her great toes are restored to her — she could she feels perform complicated dance steps if she wished to do so without missing a single harmony. The candle burns immediately in front of her, she is breathing easily from her nostrils. The room is a river of rags of light which flows slower and more slowly until it stands still. The room is a room, furnished with a table and a few chairs, with a shelf of books and some pictures, and lit with a single candle. The room is thinking its own thoughts, and Robyn is one such pleasant accustomed thought that has taken up its chair in the middle of the room's hemispheres of candle-livened light. But it is an accustomed thought like a cherished symbol with unknown potentialities, like a child who is a genius: whose gentle twin streams of warm breath mingle with the rising convection currents converging on the candle, enter the candle flame and are purified and given flame-life and ascend as into the continually renewed foliage of a tree that has always been there and always will be. The warm leafage of this tree gradually fills the whole room and Robyn is standing dressed in an armour the colour of lilies beneath a branch on which hangs a great bronze bell and a hammer. Slowly, most slowly, she reaches for the hammer handle, lifts it off its hook, draws it back slowly, and then as hard as she can strikes the bell, which howls in this language:

Nevaeh ni tra oohw Rehtaf Ruo
Eman y-ht eb dewollah
Enod eb lliw y-ht emoc modgnik y-th . . .

6

Stan Laurel is sitting with Oliver Hardy at a table. Stan wears a wing collar with tie, and a tweed jacket, and a bowler hat on his head supported by quiffs of hair like flames boiling a pot. He runs the fingers of his right hand up the back of his neck to the base of his brain and scratches the back of his head vigorously, displacing the bowler hat. He does this because of a bad-tempered remark his wife has made which neither Al Bodkin nor Greg Treviles, bosom companions on gin and whiskey, whiskey and gin, can hear because the sound track resembles the conversation of saws with hard wood. Stan's wife snaps at him again. He begins to weep, and the sound of this reaches the friends. The sound is Boo-hoo, boo-hoo. Mrs Laurel is dressed in white satin and wears a neatly bobbed wig. She is very fat. She is Oliver Hardy. The camera now shows the cause of the argument. This is the shrewish skinny wife of Oliver Hardy. She is dressed more becomingly in a figure-fitting wrap-over bodice and a long skirt, and she wears a great hat. She is expostulating vigorously with swift and agile gestures, and as she steps closer to the table at which the Laurels are seated, they cower. Oliver Hardy attempts with pudgy but tentative caresses to pacify his wife, who is Stan Laurel. She will not be soothed. She flings a final insult at Mrs Laurel, whose patience is now at an end, and who rises in imperious majesty and white satin to take physical issue with the redoubtable Mrs Hardy. Stan Laurel plucks nervously at the sleeve of her gown, as mildly to detain her, but the elegant puffed sleeve comes away in his hand. He begins whimpering again as his spouse realizes the damage and snatches the rag from his hand, raises her great ham fist. This has given Mrs Hardy a respite, and an opportunity to leave with dignity, riposting over her shoulder. She grabs the door handle and it opens, revealing a pastry-cook's deliveryman with one hand raised to knock and the other bearing a great cake under a white cloth. This is an opportunity not to be missed! Mrs Hardy snatches the cake from the astonished deliveryman, marches over to the table at which Mrs Laurel is still arguing with her husband about the destruction of her dress, and slaps the great cake, which is at least two feet across, right in Mrs Laurel's beefy face. She sits down abruptly and her chair tilts backwards. She is left sprawling on the floor with her face obliterated by the base-board of the cake, stuck to her by squashed pastry and filling. She looks like a sliced tree-trunk, with roots sprawling. Then the round base-board falls off of its own accord, and Mrs Laurel, hair and features clotted with cream, bosom and dress smothered in it, stares at the camera, no longer with flush and snapping black eyes and tiny pout, but with exhausted resignation at her messy bad luck.

7

On went the bell, chanting in the throat:

> Nevaeh ni si ti sa h'trea ni
> Daerb yliad ruo yad sith su evig
> Sessapsert ruo su evigrof *dna*
> Su tsniaga ssapsert taht meht evigrof ew sa
> Noitatpmet otni ton su deal
> Live morf su reviled tub
> Nema! Yrolg eht *dna* rewop eht modgnik eht si eniht rof

and out stepped seven black-armoured knights with differently coloured plumes waving in their helmets and black-bladed swords drawn, advancing towards the lily-armoured knight. Submissively she dropped on one knee, visor down, and to the reiterated chanting of the Russian-sounding syllables they hacked at her and hewed off her helmet and breastplate slivers that went flying into the grass. Sparks of all colours sprang from their blades as they struck, but the blows fell silently. Silently the jagged figure toppled on its right side in the grass. The seven knights stepped closer into a tighter circle and then all took a pace back with an astonished sigh. Was the armour empty? The one with a purple plume waving above his brow bent down and turned over the gorget lying there, picked up a naked girl child who wailed at the coldness and hardness of his gauntlets as he took her in both armoured hands and showed her to the others. Was this the child with genius? The group nod agreement and the leader takes the child's legs and swings her head against the tree. It bursts like a melon and little teeth stick like seeds in the smashed pulp.

Robyn's head jerked up. Snapshots of ants and butterflies swarmed in her head, then she understood that she was looking at the candle-flame and the shadows once more racing round the walls, agitated by her howls as she spoke the Lord's Prayer backwards for the third night running. The window curtains are drawn but she is aware that the lights of the town are teeming below. Her garden and Fentonluna Lane beyond her gate are dark she knows. She takes her hands from her knees and shifts slightly in her chair. Wetness in her groin tells her that her period has come. The tight pains she had scarcely been aware of as pains, but which turned into irritating clumsy acts, had gone. Instead there was a feeling of dark relief, of intense relaxation of her lower body. She licks her left forefinger and thumb, leans over and nips out the candle-flame — the execution both of the light and the shadows of the light, those running populations, makes no more sound than a brief intense hiss, and a warmth in her thumb. She sits in the perfect dark, dark without, dark within, and darkness flowing from within outwards.

8

What has he done in his nest? His pecker has cacked! It was the cake in the face. The cream. The bosom stuffed with cream. Gregory felt a trickle of it exploring his thigh. Its cool slither made him see its cloudiness. It was the light shining through old stained celluloid as the film ran out. He muttered apologetically to Al whose fair hair he could see gleaming in the twilight and took the stairs back to his room. Unzipping his trousers he looked into them and it was true. That strange film had made him come unawares, or almost unawares. The oozing of the pastry round the edge of the board had got into his eyes and made his richest filling ooze from him like a wet dream. He took up one of the paperbacks bought at the smelly little station — electrification had removed the pungent coal smells and the smuts in the eye, but the leaky gents and the horticultural packages were correspondingly intensified, and he read:

'He had eaten roast hare for breakfast, so it was not hunger that caused it, what he saw . . .' Treviles glanced at the cover. It showed a muscular god or demon with three eyes and a single horn in the middle of his forehead reaching down into a city out of which raggedly-clad girls ran. '. . . the deer on the lawn in the bright sunlight and the spotted snake coiled in its horns. Slowly the flat head wove down and held, in its tongue flickering, close by the ear of the larger animal, who tilted his head as if listening . . .' Treviles thought this very interesting, but the alcohol was making his eyes heavy and he could not keep them open. His dream continued the story without apparent transition, but was it his dream, or the dream of the writer of the paperback book, that the book existed merely to invoke in its readers? '. . . whispering advice into his ear. The man stood by his study window, watching through the thin glass, calm in the assumption of his safety. The stag with the snake wreathed in its antlers raised its head and started across the lawn towards the french windows. In a flash of lightning the man saw that the deer had human feet . . .'

Gregory started awake. He had fallen asleep with the book in front of his nose. He saw the great branched antlers of lightning, the storm massacred the deck chairs on the beach and stretched its seismic limbs over the town before he could get his eyes into focus again. He read on.

'With a trembling hand, Gregory Treviles lifted the latch of the french window . . .' with a quick sob Gregory swept the book from him like a poisonous spider. It hit the washstand mirror with an edge of its spine and the glass cracked diagonally upwards. Treviles knew without trying it that he had made himself a horned mirror, that when he looked in this glass for his reflection he would see a man furnished with branching stags' horns.

9

The paperback book had instructed her to think of great iron shackles struck off her hands and feet by sizzling bolts of lightning as she spoke the words of the Reverse Lord's Prayer. A phonetic version of this was conveniently provided. The book said that the horrid loveless edifice and burden of shalts and shalt nots would slide from her back, and she would be changed in herself by reciting this rite for the three nights before she went to bed. 'Who knows', said the book, 'what may happen? What is sure, is that something will happen. It may come to you out of the candles or out of the shadows, through the door or the window or in dreams or down the chimney, but come it will. And let it come. You will feel fear, certainly, and the degree of your fear is the measure in which you need the coming. So fear not, nobly born.'

But it was Robyn's own idea — her attention having been drawn to that time by Gregory's interest in her periods to perform the rite during her three days of clumsiness and depression that normally preceded the flow of blood. She had found — this was the third month on which this had happened — that her period started after the third invocation, at night. She felt that she was invoking the branching blood within herself, and that this perhaps was like a separate person within herself, possibly a little smaller than she was, but that might be because he was a little further away. He! certainly it was a He. And another thing was also certain: that it was not the Lord of the Christian Lord's Prayer whose apostle St Paul so despised and feared women, whose Saint Augustine learnt nothing from his first half-life of sexual freedom but that he could learn nothing from it, and should be loyal to Mother. Mother Church, a dummy made in the likeness of a woman, just as the Japanese masturbatory dummies are so made. No Church changed in itself week by week within the month, no Church bled each month. Where were the Sayings of St Mary, to tell what a woman might expect from within herself? Who split womankind up into the virgin and the whore, Mary and Mary Magdalene, and worshipped the one far off and untouchable, and made the other into a silent saint? 'Noli me tangere,' said the risen Jesus.

'Don't touch me!' Robyn could think of a good whore's reply to that — 'Go Fuck Yourself!'

And the room was alive with the tree of her blood during those times! The very first time she tried the backwards prayer, the manacles sheared off accurately in the unwelding lightning (and a spot of liquid metal flew hissing through the air and struck her high on the slope of her left breast and she could see no mark but felt the small comforting pain there for a week afterwards). Then a heavy cold sack smelling of rotting vegetation slid down her spine, slimily. The second night she was able to attend more closely to the sensation and found that it came from the small hairs, the lanugo, rippling over the shoulder-blades down to the base of her spine and joining the tickle of fear, like incontinence, in her bottom. Like two stars her nipples now began prickling and in her mind's eye she could see a line of silver down descending her back and lighting her anus and ascending again through her body until they reached her nipples, from which a faceted silver light came. In her mind's eye. The third evening the same pattern occurred, except that the plumes on her shoulders were far longer and streamed within themselves, like two great hemispheres or pinions. When she put the candle out and sat in the darkness she could hear them rustling behind her. In her mind's ear. Then the sensation sped downwards, and she knew her period had started.

But the visions of the second month were less immediately appealing. She was aware suddenly of a miniature room appearing among the candle-shadows on the wall opposite: and in this room a white dummy or doll slumped on a rickety chair, the head thrown back and hinged at the nape of the neck with large glass screws. The throat is open and the head like a lid. The neck is a black gramophone disc repeating 'Black moon, black moon'. A little head appears bawling at its whirling centre, then sinks pulling the black disc into a tunnel that descends into a world of air-raid shelters. The neck is a mine-shaft booming with the sea going down into a stone forest chattering with leaden monkeys and fruits of gold ore. The neck is a railway tunnel for ghost-trains and one is due in any moment. As the room grows larger, Robyn is staring into a large black oval mirror, and on the dressing-table beneath she finds a pair of white lace gloves, carefully laid out, her size. On the second night the room appears to Robyn again and when she touches the black surface of the mirror with her white-gloved hands it is sticky. The word 'Putrefact' comes into her mind. The third night there were no visions, only the shadows and the relaxed dark and the blood flowing after she had nipped the candle out. But her dream that night was full of colour and solid reality, the women in dresses of all colours pacing in a ring that slimmed to an ellipse and then doubled to make an 8 which folded back to a circle again. Two black women dressed in wedding gowns broke the circle carrying the oval mirror between them in white-gloved hands. They tossed it over her head like a hoop as she stood there in the centre, and she remembered no more.

10

They lived in a fair-sized stone house towards the top of the hill in the Cornish village of Petroc. At the front of their house they had a large unkempt garden which separated them from the High Street; at the back there was a single large street-door which led directly out to Fentonluna Lane. Beyond this was the manor deer-park, closed off from the outer world by a high stone wall which Fentonluna Lane followed down as far, almost, to the sea. The Manor House itself, now let out most of the year, was set higher on the town hill than they were, and more to the west.

Their house had been built by the first slatemaster of the small quarry at Petroc's Bay, who had flourished in the late eighteenth and early nineteenth century, when slate-roofing became not merely locally fashionable, and largely displaced clay tile and thatch. Accordingly the house was exceptionally solid and firmly built, the rooms were of ample size, and happily the slatemaster and his sons were unable to run to salons or neo-classical façades, so the house remained, as many Cornish houses do, being made to last out of the local stone, quite ageless, and a part of the land. If you entered by Fentonluna Lane, you stepped under an oak lintel, over an oak threshold, into a corridor that ran the whole length of the house, and showed the garden at the end of its perspective, facing east. The corridor was lined with old oak panelling, which had been allowed to keep its dark earthy glow rather than being papered over to lighten the corridor. For there were no windows to this corridor, since rooms were built left and right along its length, and only the window on the staircase landing which bent round two thirds of the way into the house gave a remote churchly light. As you had entered from high-walled Fentonluna Lane that itself was a cutting down from Manor Hill, you felt perhaps as though you were approaching into the garden from deep within the hill. It was at any rate an earth house.

Gregory had bought the house with family money. His father had been a partner in a merchant bank and he had risked equipping a vegetable haulage firm with new trucks from Germany fitted with special hydraulic-electric brakes. Following a number of appalling catastrophes on the big new motorways, a foggy carnage, legislation was forced on the Government of the time and most of the haulage firms had been forced off the road to re-equip. One of Gregory's earliest strange and sexy memories was a news photo of a car which had been rolled upon by an articulated lorry and crushed to a height of eighteen inches, with all its passengers *in situ*. In the meanwhile, railways shares went up and so did those of Clifford Treviles's cabbage haulers. The fortune, like the house Gregory eventually bought, was modest but substantial.

This good fortune in the Treviles family had been preceded by genteel poverty. Gregory's grandfather had been an emigrant pawnbroker whose shop had been bought up by a chain of jewellers with no use for the merely local skills of a backstreet moneylender. They had a tiny house in one of those same backstreets in north London, and Treviles Senior lived on the interest from the golden handshake, which was perfunctory, and the capital from selling the shop's warehouse with the shop, which had been his outright. There was just enough, therefore, to help Clifford, who was bright and won successive scholarships, to rise through the strata of class and to make quite a presentable aide in the banker's office. His cleverness with money won him a partnership.

However, his cleverness with money was a double-edged ability, as far as his family was concerned. Clifford Treviles was a man who expanded when the winds of fortune were warm, but when they sneaped, he grew crabbed — not at the office, of course, for half of monetary credit is the appearance of vitality, but at home. Then he would grow morose and mean, and most of all, he would tease. He played a nasty game with Gregory's pocket-money: he would tell the boy to wash the car and he would give him three half-crowns if he did it well within the hour. Gregory remembered giving the headlights an extra polish with Mirro which took him just three minutes over the hour — but he thought that the better the job was done the better his father would be pleased. 'No, Gregory,' his father said, 'Treviles fell three points during those three minutes, and now the stockmarket is closed and trading is finished. The car-polishing company is in liquidation. Your wages are a bad debt.'

Of course Clifford Treviles would never have dared to behave in any such way at the office, but knowing that the boy loved him enabled him to practise on him. In his relations with his clients, no such illusions entered. Moreover Clifford justified his behaviour by telling the boy that the right time to learn about money and trade was early in life.

And yet, when the real money had been made, the Treviles vitality came into its own! Nobody could be more warm and sympathetic than Clifford, or more inventive — once Gregory had seen him like this when VE — Victory in Europe, the virtual end of the Second World War — was announced over the radio. Clifford hurried Gregory and his mother and young Jon out to the car and they drove up to the streets of central London, where people, people and more people overflowed the pavements on to the roads, packing them solid. Clifford insisted in driving them through the crowds right up to the gates of Buckingham Palace to see the King and the young princesses and the Queen waving at them from the balconies. There were no other cars but only people, faces grey in the austerity lighting but all smiling and laughing and singing and forming great chains and congas and dancing along and the people gave way to the car at first willingly but later as they met the tighter-packed throngs in front of the palace they gave way with less good grace but then about a dozen angry drunken people took hold of the running-board and started to rock the car as if they would overturn it — but Clifford Treviles slid back the sunshine roof and got up on the seat and struggled his great head and shoulders through the roof and turned his shining smiling face to the people trying to overturn them and cried but with a great voice and with such vitality 'God Save the King' that all around the car took up the shout 'God Save the King!' and the whole of Buckingham Palace Yard echoed with it loudly all round and then some straggling voices began to sing the national anthem and the thousands of people took it up under the austerity lighting and there was Clifford Treviles conducting the anthem with waving arms standing on his driving seat and then the lights went on in the front balcony and out came King George with his Queen and the crowd cheered with one voice and that voice seemed, to Gregory, the voice of his father.

After that, the crowd, limp with emotion, made no more resistance to the family car's passage home than water-weed to a boat.

Gregory's mother was almost silent. She seldom spoke to the boy, or to the young man he became. There was a tacit assumption between them that nothing needed to be said. It was not that there was no love. There was love, of a magnetic kind, in that they frequently sought each other out simply to be in one another's company. Sometimes they walked together, but very little was said. Her name was Marjorie. She was not slim but not bosomy — this was how Gregory remembered her-her hair was a muted blonde colour, she dressed in blue. It was her presence, not her appearance that was important, perhaps to both of them, because she never dressed well. Later on — before Marjorie died — Gregory saw that the tacit assumption, the pact they had made between one another, was this: Clifford is good at money, but he takes most of what I can give. It was true for mother and son alike.

II

There was no need to be frightened of a book. Except that there were too many books dealing with too many subjects. Aquinas was wary of the 'man of one book' knowing that devotion to a single text sharpened a man's concentration preternaturally. In this age there were paperbacks on old subjects, new subjects, forbidden subjects, fantastic subjects, mythology, sexual lore, *romans policiers*, dictionaries of Bantu, dictionaries of Elizabethan slang, psychological case-histories, *Gray's Anatomy*, Chinese politics, demonology, alchemy, the Loch Ness Monster, *Do-It-Yourself in the Home*, *A New Life for Grown-Up Adults*, Coleridge's prose, Carlos Castañeda, Lobsang Rampa, W. B. Yeats, Giordano Bruno, *Chief Methods of Organic Synthesis*, *Lasers and Light*, *Projective Geometry*, *Dressmaking*, *The Bride of Treviles* (a Gothic Romance), *The Extra Pharmacopoeia*, *Shakespeare's Word-Play*, *Voodoo Queen*, *You Only Live Twice*, a *Guide to Tintagel*. The panorama of howling graphics and cynically-improvised visualisations of contents (the *Extra Pharmacopoeia* bore a picture of a girl in a white coat with immense cleavage caressing a test-tube; Coleridge advertised a naked woman wailing for her demon lover) fled past Treviles's inner eye like scenes from the train. He was sure that he had seen all these on the little station bookstall — he could almost see the prices in their small type.

Too many masters. For the experience of reading a book is a kind of hypnotism; you do not merely read it, you live it or dream it. And the books are so numerous and cheap that you flit from one to the other hoping to render yourself capable, somehow, of utilising all the goodies of culture the modern world has thrown up and at you (for its own purposes); and if Hermann Endenberg is right, changing your deep molecular structure as you read, with each book you read. The man of one book elects his master, dreams his master again and again, strengthens the grain of his being with his master, harmonises the symmetries of his inner bonds with his master, until all is possible to him and the little leather-bound volume that never leaves his breast pocket becomes a truly bosom friend to him, so that he never lacks conversation. A priest is like this with his breviary — he needn't actually attend church since his Master is in his book with him; and a gambler is like this with his cards, he also has his Master with him in his endless varying book of Devil's Pasteboards. But a man who reads paperbacks is racked with continual various fevers, the one as unlike the other as could be possible and still remain legible, each leaving his body alternately weakened and strengthened as though one were to temper a piece of metal in custard, treacle, urine, eggs, jam, bathwater, mud, clay, wedding-cake, shit, mayonnaise, lemon sorbet, autumn leaves, Cornish cream, rose-petals, Loch Ness, and a police inspector.

Treviles, realising he would not now sleep, reached into his grip for another paperback.

12

Robyn is Gregory's stepdaughter, which is not allowed in the degrees of kinship listed at the back of the book of common prayer. She had turned the room that was the oldest part of the house into her study, in which she sat at nights reading and writing, not at all lonely for Gregory, but looking forward to his return. Notwithstanding the rites she performed in this room, which were after all only the simplest form of taboo-breaking and self-hypnotism, the easiest possible way of turning herself inside-out, she had no fear of being alone in it or in the house. Because of the rites, she was growing to believe, she had no fear. People invariably fear lonely or sacred places, as Coleridge aphorised, because some 'frightful fiend/Doth close behind him tread'. Robyn did not feel that her back was unprotected, that some spider or hand would land suddenly on her shoulder, some chin lodge on it and turning: the face! or some knife ease under her shoulder-blade. If a person walked close behind her, then she was sure that person was a friend — why this should be after breaking the Christian taboo, she was not sure. At other times, if she thought about it at all as she was climbing the stairs to the great slate bed in the master-bedroom (the slate bedstead erected by the original slatemaster, and so heavy that it was supported on a special pillar sunk into the foundations) it was maybe because her back was protected by the great wings that rustled in the dark.

13

If you take a glass of cold water, and pour it into the sea at Fentonluna Point, and then wait six months to ensure that your glass of water is thoroughly mixed into all the waters of all the oceans (the prevailing current which makes bathing so dangerous at the dark moon and the spring tide will take your droplet of water out into the Irish Sea and it will meet up with the Gulf Stream and in due course mix with the entire waters of the Atlantic before it turns left at Africa for the Indian Sea and the Pacific) and you have marked this water: let it perhaps be a glass of tritium oxide T_2o, an isotope of hydrogen, or let it be a glass of water that you just know; then if you travelled to stay with Arthur C. Clarke on the island of Ceylon, now known as Sri Lanka, and if after dinner with Arthur, politely wiping your lips on your sarong, you requested leave 'I just have something I must check up on?' and walked out on Lobsang Rampa point and drained your glass of Ceylon brandy and dipped the vessel at this point some 3000 miles away from Fentonluna, and stared into your glass — you would then be able to count out no less than 100,000 of your original marked molecules of water in this new Ceylonese glass. That is how numerous molecules are. That is how small molecules are.

Or, alternatively, if you enlarged one adenosine triphosphate molecule from the protoplasm of one cell from the tip of your tongue to the size of the slatemaster's house in Fentonluna Lane, and a great spectacle this would be like a solid chord of music, something between a symphony and a fleet of Rolls-Royces, or something between a brass band and the laboratory of Dr Frankenstein, if you enlarged the molecule to this size and allowed your body to expand in scale, then the cell from which you took this molecule would be the size of the earth, and your body would be the size of the galaxy with its billion billion suns where the light takes a billion years to pass from one end to the other.

Treviles opened his paperback, a popular American work on biophysics, at random. The random page spoke to his thoughts, thus: 'In your body you have about five octillion atoms . . . this number is represented by the number five followed by twenty-seven zeroes. In order to grasp this number imagine the ordinary lead shot that hunters use in their cartridges. A million of these will fill the ordinary size of coffin. A billion of these will fill, and sink, the liner QE2. A quadrillion of these will fill all the room space in New York. A sextillion of lead shot will fill all the seas of the earth and cover the land masses to a depth of two feet. An octillion of shot will do this to one million and a quarter planets the size of earth. Such an action on the part of irresponsible gods would upset the balance of gravitational forces in the galaxy. It is not possible to predict what might then happen, but at a good guess the disc that is the Milky Way would be profoundly affected, as a quoit made with an unevenly distributed weight would fly in a limp and lame fashion, precarious as a duck whose wings are brittle with the winter cold; or as the uneven curling stone treacherously crushes the toes of its scotsmen; or as in a flying saucer when a heavy mass of freight slips in the hold. Prediction falters because that one and a quarter million of planets is not the sum of the possible planets in the Milky Way, the likely number is several million times greater, and it would be impossible to ensure an even distribution of lead-shotted (or as one might say lead-shat) planets. So the Milky Way, our galaxy, would begin to wobble and fall into unimaginable abysses, not space as we conceive it on our minute infinitesimal scale, but space curved and twisted and turned inside out in ways that we do not yet know. And yet in its falling, the galaxy would spend such aeons of time as would allow of the evolution of a new conscious life-form and a new space technology based on the properties of the atom of soft Saturnian lead, found in such quantities on certain planets in our galaxy . . .'

14

Robyn, the bride of Treviles, contemplated the bridegroom's portrait done in oils by Al Bodkin. She watched the candlelight lap over the picture and wondered why Bodkin had posed him with a skull in his hand. Why he had painted Treviles, whom she did not find at all theatrical a person, as Hamlet. The tones of the portrait were muted and the technique employed thick, swirling strokes, as though the picture had suddenly materialised through being beaten up by an eggwhisk. The face was strong, though idealised. Robyn knew that Al had worked on the face for days of sitting until he had done a drawing he felt was right — then he transferred it mechanically to an oval left blank above the figure's torso, which had taken him an afternoon to do, and looked it.

Treviles was dressed in deeply open white shirt and black doublet. Red hair curled on his chest, on his chin, on his head. His beard jutted, his spine erect, his head held determinedly, he looked like the portrait of King Edward VII on the Players' cigarette packets. 'This is how a patient in full transference sees him,' exclaimed Robyn aloud, 'nobody ever looked like this! It's like a political portrait, one made for propaganda purposes, or the postcard of a saint, tuppence coloured. Though there isn't much colour there. Black and white of the clothes, ivory of the skull, the grey eyes, skin-tints, and red hair.' Then she noticed something new to her in the picture. The skull, which was small and delicately formed, like a woman's, wore, lankly plastered across its brow, a lock of red. Red hair, just a snippet, as though somebody who kept such a relic, perhaps coiled in a locket or small cedar-wood box, had taken it out for the occasion, laid it on the skull's brow and slicked it down with a little water or spit. Robyn crossed to the electric light switch and snapped it on. Yes, the hank of red hair was really there, on the skull, the candlelight had not imagined it. Robyn felt her own hair stirring on her scalp, and for the very first time in her recollection she was uneasy in the long dark corridor of the slatemaster's house. Then her anger began. 'The bastard! that shit-sipping bastard Al.' She thought how the clean virtue of the priest of an extinct religion cast a very dirty shadow. Then the anger which was coloured like whips and iron turned inside out and the knapsack was full of hot salt water that felt its way down her cheeks to the corners of her mouth as she wept at the macabre insult to her dead mother, Mamie.

15

The starry spaces swept together and became his body. Across his chest lay *The Orchestra of the Universe.* He rubbed his eyes and swung his legs over the side of the bed. The mirror was still cracked and the offending mystery story was still on the floor. He opened his case and took out a bag of apples. Selecting one, he rubbed the fruit to polish and clean it on the sleeve of his shirt. He took a fold of the light blue material and twirled it inside the stalk-navel and the calyx-mouth. This action left a greasy brown stain on the shirting. "What molecules', he grumbled, 'what molecules. What can we learn from an alphabet designed to kill insects?' He ran warm water and then cold water over the apple. Apple-scent rose. Under his fingertips, the skin felt supple and waxy. 'The messages from what I touch . . .' He took a great bite and the juice fizzed like sharp sparkling cider through his teeth that relished the snap they had just taken, and felt strong and white. He bared his teeth in a strong white grin. According to his grandfather's watch it was four o'clock in the morning.

Riffling through *The Orchestra of the Universe* he found no mention of the cosmic experience with lead shot. It was a dream, or it was a form of hypnotism. Call it hypnagogic — just as when one falls asleep one may hear a beautiful cadenza on the piano, the squark of a parrot, or feel bolts of silk drawn through one's hands, so a self in him had been thrown into violent inventive activity by a paragraph, plain words from one of the too numerous and convincing masters of the modern world — this one a biophysicist. He remembered the constant news flashes when the dreadful leaden rain began falling on planet earth and the television pictures of skyscrapers crumbling under incessant pitting by small round shot falling at the acceleration of a hailstorm. The bunker from which he watched these broadcasts with his wife in the armchair beside him (he had forgotten her name) and the twins fast asleep in their cots had slowly crushed to a concrete sandwich over a day and a night, but the first abrupt snapping of the reinforced concrete at the lintels had jammed the sliding steel doors so there had been no escape for them. He had shot her and smothered the two babies, then, weak from the heat and the smell of blood, he shot himself. Whereupon he was a leaden planet on which the shot had melted and run into the crust and the land sterile of all life was rising in mountain peaks upon which the vaporised seas rained until there was a planet of small islands and no nations, a total archipelago. 'This is what I do to my patients,' he thought, 'I give them a phrase or image from their dream which returns them to their dream, immerses them in their total being, as hard irregular crystals are dissolved to form a solution in which all movements and reactions are possible, which is then concentrated so that new lattices of more perfect order and strength with new properties and abilities are formed'.

'But I am dissolving from too much proximity I dare say not into myself but into everybody else. A hypnotist like Rasputin would make me one of his avenue of living statues to amuse the Csarina; a hypnotist like Freud could impose with mastery his own conflicts on me so that I would experience a release of energy of my own in solving them for him — or at least giving him a mirror in which he could see himself clearly'.

'Now this is wrong! I am not wax! I am Gregory Treviles! These books, these psychologists, these film comedians are not so much imposing their will on me, though no doubt they would wish to, but rather they are asking questions, not just of me but of anybody who encounters their insane projects. They are saying with one voice, "Please, I am mad, I am in despair, life has no meaning, I only like throwing custard pies at my wife, I only like making money, I only like picking my nose"; and with the other voice "Ah Yes. It's quite plain. I can see it all. This is the secret of the universe."

'Surely my secret is no secret. I am amazed by what they say, and I become hypnotised. That is all to the good, for there is nobody to say to me in this experiment, "When you awake you will forget all that has happened to you". I can remember quite clearly, too clearly, what has happened to me, and it has a meaning. It must have a meaning, since the life in these people (of whom of course I am one) is getting a spontaneous reply from the life in me! And vice versa. It is life talking back to life in life's own language: creative forms, strange beings, ghosts and gods; poem-language, and I, if I want to be a doctor, or a poet, that I is just the watcher of the changes, who must endure his own imagination and his protean changes of form, vertigoes of time, abysses and deformations of space, patiently, and without recourse to tranquillisers, noticing but above all believing in that which is not expected.'

Having delivered this speech to the psychological congress of one red-bearded man wearing horns in the mirror, Dr Treviles poured himself a small glass of whiskey, drank it down, pulled off his shirt, stared for a moment at his fortyish-year-old tits in the cracked mirror, got into bed in his underpants, laid his warm hands comfortably on his penis, and went to sleep.

16

Robyn was astounded at such a bizarre insult to her mother, Treviles's wife Mamie (for Mary), who, like Gregory and herself, possessed a head of flaming red hair. To paint a man holding his wife's skull! Jealousy? Or did the great medium of oil paint, holding its seances between the canvas and the hand of the artist, like a planchette, spell out some necessary message or warning about her father-lover? Why had she never noticed the unpleasant lick of red hair across the ivory skull before this evening? Mamie had been cremated so perhaps this skull was also made of burnt bone, or it was a skull of ash, fragile as a dried rose, held together with love's mucilage, sculpted in some insane act of devotion by the bereaved husband. Or it had made itself out of ash, gathering itself out of the sea air. (Mamie's ashes were handed over to them both in a thin metal urn. Inside the urn, a polythene bag. Inside the bag, grey ashes, that clung together in lumps, as though moist.

Robyn could still see Gregory absently rubbing these between finger and thumb to smooth the lumps out before scattering his wife's ashes off Fentonluna Point. This they did, in full sunlight, at teatime, at four in the afternoon, since Petroc collectively still took tea, and the was deserted. A stiff breeze blew out to sea; Gregory took the end of the bag in his right hand, holding it closed with his left, then with an abrupt choking gesture flung out with his right so that the ashes flew into the wind like a puff of bonfire smoke. She could not look at her stepfather's face, but believed he was crying. The puff of smoke unfolded on the wind, swashed and swiftly erased, but not before its fading billows had made with a hill of red pines on the opposite shore, a twisting red-haired acre-face of Mamie.) This impulse of Mamie to return and alight on Treviles's palm — why couldn't Al have painted the more-regenerated woman, a tiny red-haired nude standing upright and triumphant on the palm of his hand? Or perhaps, since she was now part of the earth they trod on, painted Treviles standing on dead, nude Mamie's palm? Was it an ash skull, or a scab skull that grew constantly from some wound the painter had conceived in Treviles's right hand, the hand that Robyn as a child remembered watching strike Mamie's cheek (singing in her skull) three times, the two of them standing on the hearth rug in front of a cheerful fire?

Al Bodkin had never got at her like this before. Not in any way at all. She thought him a fool, in the way that she thought all Christian clergymen were fools, since their Pauline doctrines commanded hygienic married sex, or none at all, preferably, and their God of light was unable to look into the darkness of women. Her doctrinal disgust was manifold, but her personal contempt of Bodkin was specific. She thought him pretentious and ungifted. He was dilettante. Painting, for instance. A hobby, executed with great gestures of privilege, meditation, and silence; but he would drop it in an instant for some new toy. Not long after he had met Treviles, a sudden evolution turned him into an expert on dream interpretation. Painting then to him was a mere disguise of his true feeling, and the dream told all. He would closet himself with distressed parishioners and breezily interpret their dreams in the name of Christ by the hour. He was a friendly man, so for the main part this did little harm. However, after one of his sessions with a member of the local hippie community, the young man had walked straight out and strangled his baby. There was a scandal, Bodkin's liberality — which seemed genuine, but which Robyn, maliciously, preferred to regard as *laissez-faire*, an unwillingness to face up to the possibility that he, Bodkin, could ever make a life decision and just be wrong for once — in allowing the hippies to camp among the gravestones since the council would not allow them to use the proper camping sites (and the graveyard tap for watering grave-flowers provided their ablutions) misfired badly, and council was the victor over church. Bodkin's sparse congregations halved. The Bishop of Cornwall came down and talked privately to his errant priest for five solid hours, and Robyn did not think that there was any interpretation of dreams at that session. After that Rev. Bodkin was never known to discuss dreams again, not with his parishioners at least, though he sometimes did with Gregory, and all his parish interviews were given with the door half open and Mrs Bodkin in the kitchen. It was then that he went back to painting, which did not require him to open his mouth, and it was then that Treviles sat for the portrait.

She also hated his lank fair hair, his sharp nose, his Malcolm Muggeridge voice and smarmy Christian optimism. Above all — and this strained ordinary civilised politeness to an acquaintance to the utmost — his foul breath. Mrs Bodkin's breath — Alicia's breath-smelt foul also, but was not in the same class as Alec's, nor did it reach across a tea-table when she spoke. The two children's breath was as sweet-smelling when they spoke, as most children's is, but no doubt, as soon as puberty was achieved, whatever had gone wrong with their parents' organs would fail in their own also.

But now Alexander Bodkin had stolen her imagination with his visual jibe at the man he supposedly respected, and of whom he had painted an otherwise obsequious portrait. She imagined him dining at their table, and then, in between the fish and the meat, she would get up and turn off the electric light, and the neat clergyman with the plastered not-quite-fair hair would disappear with the godly light, and in his place would be sitting a shit-eating dog-face whose features were fitfully illuminated by the phosphorescence of his foul breath.

17

Grey-eyed Athene told him how to do it, pretending to be the fair-haired charioteer Iolaus as they careered down Fentonlerna Lane towards the unfathomable Lernaean swamp. 'Hold your breath,' she advised, the goddess' eyes watching him out of the man's face, 'for its poisonous breath will render you weak and helpless.' Together they drove the hydra out of its lair with burning arrows, and at the moment the goddess stepped out of the body of his companion (whose bolt eyes were now blue with fear, who turned and whipped the chariot away), he glimpsed among the hundred heads writhing on their snaky necks, the steady grey-eyed gaze of the central head, the immortal head, the cheeks of which were made of gold. It was his task to sever this part and bury it under a stone, though it might still hiss and gnash there for all time, but as he fought towards it, gold falchion blazing, for each head that he severed three grew in their place. Out of the corner of his eye he glimpsed a blaze of fire. 'Good man!' Al Iolaus had fired the brushwood. Now he could cauterise the raw stumps as he lopped the heads and so he would be at the golden centre.

As he wounded it, the hydra throve, crying hallelujas. Blood jetted sevenfold from the lopped necks, taking the colours of the rainbow as it met the air. Where it fell, coloured flowers sprang up. As he severed heads, the heads that fell unfolded into fruiting vines that took quick root. Threefold heads replaced each head that fell, as if anxious to make more flowers, more fruit. Accordingly, the new, awakened heads smiled down at the exhausted hero benevolently crying 'Halleluja! Top me! Halleluja!' The blood fell on to his clothes, on to his shirt, and the shirt-pattern flowered into real blooms on real trellises, on to his trousers and they were instantly set thick with a piling of full-sized penises that pissed golden urine, and where they pissed, buttercups raised their faces to the sky. Stepping naked from his living clothes the hero also raised his face to heaven and cried 'Athene! Au secours!'

Instantly a neck snaked round the pummel of his sword, snatched it from him, and decapitated him with a single stroke, teeth grinding.

I came to the red grove believing that the head was still there, resting deep within the shrubbery like a boulder matted with fern or red turf. Part the tufty beard gently, and there are teeth, still grinding, eyes, still watching. The legends say that the ravenous raw stump feeds on earth and stones. There are tracks eaten into the ground weaving between the trees in figures of eight. This is where the head has been feeding and shifting its pasturing position.

It sits on its neck in the grove of red trees. The mouth curses the hydra, since the mouth is not used for eating. Around the head-grove, the herds of deer feed on the red shoots and the buck mounts the doe's russet haunches.

The head excretes by growing its hair and its beard and by weeping sand. It has wound its hair and its beard all around the trees of the grove like wool on a skein in figures of eight. The grove is a knot of red hair, tied into itself like an old woman's bun, flaming red on the outside but peppered — with white further in, as the head ties itself into tighter and lighter knots, weeping, eating rocks and earth, and gnashing sparks from its flinty teeth.

The legends tell how a person must come, a very ordinary person, if possible a silly person because once the head has tied itself to a standstill, its teeth-gnashing will become so intense and incessant and concentrated to a single place that the grove will burst into flames and release such a cloud of poison on the land that all will be laid waste. So I am come, a Christian clergyman, Bodkin by name, perfectly aware that God has given me a silly pointed nose and silly-ass fair hair that lies lankly on my silly scalp and a voice like Malcolm Muggeridge and doggy friendly manners and an optimism which rises as I grow more frightened, and a lot of silly little talents and enthusiasms none of which amounts to much, and very bad breath through no fault of my own, though it might be my wife's cooking.

One of the things I was very keen on a while ago was scything, which I thought both very useful, if the grass were long that is, very graceful, and good exercise. So I brought my scythe and my hone with me, to cut down the red grove, and rescue the head. The red hair was very tough since it was made of rock and earth, if the legends spoke true, and I worked all day cheerfully scything and honing frequently, using spit on my whetstone like old farmer Bayard showed me. I sat down and poured myself a cup of tea from my thermos and contemplated with considerable satisfaction the inroads I had already made. Pride will have a fall! I realised suddenly, and dropped hot tea on myself as it dawned on me, that I must scythe above the height of a head! Otherwise I would kill the head myself; his rescuer would be the death of his hero. So when I resumed work I cut the hair with even strokes upward, beginning above neck-and-head height at each new swathe so that I would not injure what I had come to find, or scythe through an eyeball into a brain. But having been for so long without blood, would not the eyeball be glass and the brain a wrinkled coral? At any rate, having completed each row, I felt very carefully about in the long stubble, expecting at any moment to feel teeth among the hair.

I forced myself not to hurry. Perhaps the result of the head's winding itself in an immobile pattern would be that it would travel downwards, for ever, through bedrock, through coal, through oil, through molten magma, through the rock of rocks, the original green olivine, down into the iron core of the planet that swings in liquid like the clapper of a bell. As my hero descended the excretion of his hair and whiskers would rise into the grove and increase its height and composition, so that it would become a banded mountain of terraces of different materials, like Dante's stratified purgatory thrown up by the fall into the centre of the earth of Satan. And then again the head might easily be unable to digest bedrock, and its sparking teeth would give it light only in its caverns and no heat, so that all I should find would be a crater like a well the diameter of a head and I would haul out of it by the long-braided hair a dead and quiet skull like a bucket.

The next day, after a curiously unrefreshing slumber in my sleeping-bag, I removed my god-collar once again and set to. I delved inwards with careful strokes, like a man cutting the cables of gigantic spider-webs stacked layer upon layer like blood-soaked gramophone records. As I released them from their bonds of hair, the dead trees crashed to the ground. There was no soil for their roots. I recognised the gnarled wood, and my guess was confirmed by a layer of broad leaves lying on the ground. This was a grove of vines that had taken root like ordinary trees! By the second sunset I had scythed in the stack a cavern the size of a woodland cottage, and a fresh breeze was blowing the hair that I had cut free into great tumbling red-and-white globes like tumbleweed that ran away over the plain towards the setting sun making its new glory in the clouds. A final gust toppled the last vine and rolled the remaining hair off to the west. In the centre of the red stubble, dark against the sun, I saw a small ancient boulder, and in pulsations, a phosphorescent light shone in its clicking teeth.

My knees were weak but I walked boldly towards the apparition and saw how the wind blew into its hair and parted it revealing now the sparking teeth, now the glinting eyes. I saw too that where the seven great vines had rooted, all springs were glittering like fountains. I lurched forwards suddenly, wrenching my back! I was thigh-deep in mud. The springs were turning the grove back into water, the ancient Leunaean swamp, which the Emperor Nero had attempted to sound and found bottomless. At the centre, the object of my quest bobbed like a football in a swimming-pool, I saw its eyes imploring me as the mud rose. But I was sinking also. However much I stretched I could not reach him! But then with a desperate effort I pulled my body out of the mud and threw myself forward towards the head, like a goalkeeper diving to save a goal, snatched my prize and not stopping to think threw myself full length backwards. By turning and wriggling very swiftly and not allowing myself the luxury of the thought that I might sink, for I certainly would if I stopped, I soon made dry land, plastered with mud, black, unrecognisable, like a footballer in a thunderstorm, an odour of twilight chilling me. I went to one of the seven springs, and carefully washed mud off my hero's face and out of his beard, and tore a square from the tail of my shirt, and laid him gently on the left-hand side of his face, and washed myself as best I could.

Then, wet and chilled though I was (but remembering after all it was what I came for) I lifted the head respectfully by its hair to my mouth and whispered my greetings into its ear.

The lips writhed, but no sound came. I bent down and soaked the tail of my shirt in the spring water, to moisten the lips. As I did so, I felt a sharp pain in my hand. It had touched the edge of the severed neck, and the digestive juices had burnt me. Then I heard a faint belch of air, and a soft gasp. The severed oesophagus and windpipe had learned to gulp air upwards, and form the sounds into very soft but liquid speech.

'Take me to the rising ground to the east, Alexander. If the young deer with the two great horns and the seven short tines between them comes, give me to him. If he does not come, throw me out into the very centre of the marsh that I may cover my face again with the silent mud, for what then will come upon mankind will be better not seen.'

With the head swinging like a holy lantern in my grasp I climbed the tussocky hill in the gathering darkness. I could see that a crowd of figures had gathered above me, and as I came up to them I saw that it was a herd of does, of hornless deer. As I neared the herd parted and through them paced a young stag with two splendid horns that must have been all of five feet long. Between these horns a separate growth sprang on the crown of his head, seven soft velvet-covered knobs. As he stalked towards me, I held out the head towards him. He came close, and I looked straight into his eyes, for he was the height of a man. They were deep and brown, they were like deep pools of clear water lined with moss. Then he knelt on his two forelegs, lowering his head towards me. I lifted the jagged neck of the hero's head over the seven knobs of the deer's crown, and they fitted exactly. The head rested between the two horns on the crown of the stag's head, and as the latter rose to its feet from its knees the hair fell aside from the head's face and for the first time I had a direct sight of the aged countenance. It was grey and hard and the eyes were bolted from their sockets. As I watched a tone of blood crept into the cheeks and into the flesh and the sockets relaxed and the eyelids blinked and the eyes saw me and smiled and the stag turned and the stag wheeled and the stag galloped away swiftly into the darkness followed by his does and I was left with the memory of a face.

That was how I decided to take up oil painting again. So that I could make a portrait of that face.

18

Tonight alone in the great slate bed it was like spreading out mattress and sheets on a wide family tomb in a silent church. Robyn had grown up in this house. But she had never before considered the skull of her mother. She had been a very young child when her mother had met Gregory in the Army Hospital. Robyn could remember Mamie in her grey uniform with the red belt, the shoulder-tabs with the three silver 'pips' fastened to them, the white headscarf covering the red hair bending to kiss her and turning away with a rustle of starched skirts. She remembered the sound of the car and its headlights reflected on the bedroom ceiling as her mother drove away on night duty. She supposed that somebody in the house looked after her when her mother was away, but she had no idea who it was. She felt quite secure. One evening her mother brought this tall doctor back for a cup of coffee. Robyn remembered him looking quite frightened and clean-shaven, and his nervous eyes scared her and yet they were kindly at the same time, and confident, like a sentry on the alert. He too wore three pips — later she remembered a single crown — but a khaki uniform. She recalled her fascination with the stiffness of the khaki twill in his jacket and trousers, against the agility and swift expressive folds of the khaki shirting that showed on either side of his tie in the vee of his uniform. It was like a muddy stream that flowed over much country — his face was noted, but not then watched, once she felt confident — it was the roughness like coarse sand of the cloth he wore on the outside, and the silty fineness of that which was closer to his skin.

Nor did she remember that his hair was that flaming red colour which is such a feature of their three lives, or their two lives and their one death. The brilliantine which at that time — the early fifties — was a feature of men's dress, smarming and glistening and darkening the hair, was very likely responsible. Robyn remembered asking Gregory about it as a child.

'Daddy, was your hair always red?'

'Darling, I like you calling me Daddy, but my name is Gregory really.'

'Greggy, was your hair always red?'

'No dear, it went red shortly after I met your mother. Before that it was brown, like the cushion here.'

'Oh. Why did it go red when you met Mamie?'

'Because I loved her.'

'Why?'

'The colour of love is red.'

'Why?'

'Don't just say Why ducky. Try and think what I said.'

'Why?'

'I love you.'

Then she asked him about it again. She was teenaged, and in her first year at Cambridge. They had been talking together, Mamie, Robyn and Gregory about the inconvenient fact that though she had won not just a State Scholarship but an Open Scholarship to her college and could therefore theoretically support herself, because her stepfather's income was quite high, she was debarred from receiving any money from these (except that her college allowed her £100 a year as a scholar for lodging and buttery), and she was thus dependent on him. She disliked being dependent, she disliked his having to see her book bills as much as her dress bills. So they quarrelled, and she defied him to disown her. He told her that she was a dreadful little whore, physically, emotionally and intellectually, but the thought of the Cambridge intellectual whores all three knew, sitting at the feet of fashionable dons, was too much for them, and they burst out laughing. 'Nobody with your colour hair could be just an intellectual whore, Robyn,' said Treviles. 'Nor you. Or you, Mamie. Greg, I do remember you with dark brown hair, I think, when Mummy used to bring you back to the flat.' 'During my call-up . . . well Robyn, you may not believe this, but my hair went this colour shortly after I met your mother. I was a national serviceman. Since I was already a doctor, they made me an officer very quickly, as they did all the qualified men on the call-up. I was working for my D.P.M. since I wanted to practise as a psychiatrist, but it was the first time I had ever worked with mental patients. 'Do you remember,' speaking to Mamie, 'the tall man with the fine brow, noble cranial arch, who had the leucotomy?' 'He was called Whitehead.' 'Whitehead. I used to talk to him. I couldn't do anything for him, but he liked talking. The medical board wanted him to have a leucotomy, his noble brow, his frontal lobes disconnected, and I opposed this. Very strongly. He looked like Shakespeare! But I had no other treatment to suggest. They called him up before the Board, and he clinched the deal himself by explaining that he could not endure his desire to strangle his two babies. So they leucotomised him. At that time they had not worked out the technique of approaching the brain with a cautery through the eye-socket so that no scar was visible. Instead they made saw-cuts into the temples and wiggled about with a bistoury. Hit or miss. The survival rate was about 70 per-cent. I watched the operation, did not assist. Afterwards, when he had recovered from the immediate effects of surgery, I met him walking in the grounds. He had a black beret on his head and two strips of sticking plaster down his temples. He recognised me and this was a relief. He came up to me. "Doctor," he said, "thank you. I feel so much better." I tried to be casual, but I felt my face grow red from shame. Conan Doyle in one of his stories describes a man with a stroke as "that great brain no more use than a cap full of porridge". I said something encouraging to him and went about my business — I remember I had to talk to an RSM, a fine-looking bronzed man with many years of service, who had burst into tears on the parade-ground, and was in the process of being rehabilitated, which meant being kept into hospital until his retirement papers came through — but the blush stayed on my face. It was still there when I sat down with the RSM and he asked me whether I had caught the sun. I asked the skin man to look at it and he gave me an injection and told me to lie down, but the blush stayed on my face for the rest of the month.' 'Gregory, this isn't a shaggy dog story?' 'No! Mamie, you remember.' Mamie laughed and nodded. 'I'd just been posted to the hospital and I remember doing ward round with this young officer with the scarlet face. I thought him a good doctor, but he'd have to do something about his complexion, or his blood pressure, or both.' 'The blush went, of course. I was seeing red! I caught Mamie with her white cap off and I was amazed at the red belt, red tabs, red hair. I expect the blood drained from my face. I noticed later that my hair was growing lighter, auburn, and I got a lot of chaffing because everybody thought I was dyeing it to impress the nurses, or (as they soon saw) the Nurse. In a month or two it was the colour you see now.' 'I thought that as some people are said to go white-haired overnight from shock,' said Mamie, ('Authenticated,' said Treviles, 'I have the references'.) 'Gregory went red. First from shame, and then from passionate devotion.' 'I know that my ideas crystallised at that time, and I began planning my thesis for the D.P.M.' And they sat on in the front room watching the garden darken into evening.

In Robyn's ancient study, in that part of the house already standing when the first slatemaster sold tiles to Roman citizens, on a tall shelf among several such books, a fat redbound typescript: 'The Attainment of Deep Trance Hypnotic conditions in Hysteric and Psychotic Subjects, with an Appendix on the Use of Jung's Technique of Active Imagination Under Trance Conditions.'

19

As soon as he woke, Gregory started writing down the hydra dream in which he had been Al. The maid came with the morning tea as he finished the last sentence 'So that I could make a portrait of that face'. At breakfast the dining-room was nearly empty. Most of the delegates had already left. Gregory sat down with Al Bodkin, who had tucked his napkin into his dog-collar as if to conceal his vocation from all watchers while he spread marmalade thickly on secular bread with lustful pleasure. 'I dreamt I was you last night,' said Gregory. Al blushed, and swallowed his mouthful. 'Good morning!' He always said good morning, just as he always Said 'In the name of the Father etc.' before preaching. This annoyed Gregory. Alec was a liturgical clockwork, with an almost unmarked face, and a yellow cap of hair like an alarm clock with a brass bell. 'That's nice,' continued Bodkin, 'I'd like to dream that I was you,' his blush growing fierier. Treviles was aware that he had spoilt Alec's breakfast by embarrassing him. Shortly this cleric would tell a joke or make a quip, then he'd start laughing, and both of them would start laughing, and nothing more would be said for the sound of embarrassed laughter deliberately sought as armour and defence. 'Tell me, Alexander,' Gregory went on, 'have you given up painting entirely?' 'Since I painted you.' 'Why?' 'Too much to do. You gave me ideas about dreams, and I wanted to use them to help the people in the parish.' 'But you're a Christian. What have you to do with dreams? As your psychotic Paul says, your God is light. What has he to do with things that come in the dark? You don't look for dreams in the sunlight, in broad day! At night you are the female, and the universe comes to make love to you.' 'Love, yes. Make love, no. God is love.' 'Sex made us. God made us. Ergo, God is sex.' 'Gregory, I was enjoying my breakfast,' (sadly). 'Making love to toast and marmalade. Do you try not to love the taste of Jesus at communion? He's not very tasty, in my experience.' (Sharply) 'I try to transform my instincts, Gregory.' 'Yes,' said Gregory, 'I'm afraid you do.' 'I worry about you Gregory. Sometimes I think you're a bit mad.' 'Oh, that's a professional risk!' 'Sex-mad, Gregory.' 'Is there any other kind?' 'I wouldn't be a patient of yours, Gregory.' 'I agree with you, but among so many others, who are we to differ. Anyway, Alexander, you're too useful to me as a friend. I can be as angry as I like with you and you don't mind. You don't seem to mind. I can be as cross as I like.' 'Yes, it is my Cross,' said Alec Bodkin, smugly.

20

The horned god of fire, with seven tongues, Agni, brother to Indra, glittering god of melted butter, licker up of the sacrifices, thrice-born, once as the sun, twice as the lightning, and thrice as the flame kindled in the priestess's hand, in the candle.

Candles were central to Robyn's meditation techniques, or magic techniques — she called them by different ideas according to her mood, according to whether she wished to bring something about, like her period, or to learn something, or to refresh her body from sleep at the beginning of the day, as now. Her morning exercise was a form, a very simple form (for it was her opinion, and Gregory's, that the true things were things that everybody could understand and experience; however complex they sometimes appeared, as dreams sometimes did, nevertheless the dreamer underwent them without conscious effort) of Agni Yoga. All effective magical (or meditatory) practices are to be found in the Yoga systems: Robyn's fascination with candles, which she found for herself, but which can hardly be ignored in any holy institution that burns candles at altars or saints' images, is known as Trataka. Hatha Yoga, the form of Yoga most often taught and practised in the West, involves bodily exercises. There is also Jnana Yoga, some of whose exercises appeared to Robyn to resemble Zen practices, since the aspirant would imagine very vividly and with every sense some object and event, and then with a stroke of the mind cancel it, saying 'not this, not this'. In doing so he or she found the true self, the user, behind the appearance. Robyn had read one book she remembered which to her produced this insight. It was *In the Country of the Skin,* the first prose work of a poet called Redgrove. It consisted of small, rapidly created universes which the poet then destroyed by creating another such universe as rapidly, and again, and so on, until he discovered the users of the universe which to him were a trinity: a white man, a black woman, and a sandy-haired man.

Bhakti Yoga was 'union by love'; Karma Yoga by service; Mantra Yoga by poetry or other powerful words, as she had sometimes felt in lectures by Endenberg, a unity of audience and lecturer and wooden seats and ancient sky outside. It was the clarity of his voice combined with the power of his ideas, and the rhythm of this clear voice, and an attitude in him which was in a way like radar-seeking, for to begin a lecture he would speak with long pauses his head cocked and the pauses to do with the sound of the words and not their sense, as though he were sending out vibrations and listening to what they invoked; then he would gather to a normal speed of talking and sound and sense fused together; it was then that audience and lecturer became one organism united less by words than by a nervous flow. Endenberg had a large independent research laboratory in Hampshire, and a practice in London, in Queen Anne Street, but he was also Visitor to An Cuntellow, the University of Cornwall, as Gregory was. Robyn had applied for an assistant lecturer's job in the Department of Molecular Biology, but was not sure that she would like it if she got it. Gregory favoured the idea; he said there was no other place of learning in the world that promised so much from interdisciplinary studies. Thus Endenberg lectured in the Chemistry School at Ruan Minor and on psychotherapy at Tintagel College (the old Arthur's Table Hotel, high on the northern cliffs). Gregory's chief seminar as Visitor was held in the Department of English Language and Literature that used the old premises of the Penycumgwic Institute of Art, which moved to Camborne when the University was formed; his seminar was on 'Practical Poetry' and he took as his theme and motto Rimbaud's saying:

one must, I say, become a seer,
make oneself into a seer

Agni Yoga was like making oneself into a super-candle! The technique was to imagine a small and intensely white light six inches above the crown of your head. You then let this white light enlarge and stream down through all your body, like a shower of radiation or a drenching white thunderstorm where the rain and the lightning had become one. She had once seen a variety act on the stage with comic decorators falling about with their paint and their bowls all in white boiler suits that became rainbow coloured. At the climax the immaculately red-bloused and black-skirted and high-coiffed black-haired lady of the house had flung open the door to complain again about the noise, knocking aside the ladder of a trestle on which was set a large plastic bucket of white paint which fell down over her head and drenched her, white. This brought a roar of laughter that was also shocked and because shocked also refreshed, and Robyn thought that this would be a very refreshing thing to happen, after coiffing and dressing so neurotically to find oneself inevitably equal with the messy comics whose only aggressing was to fling paint like blood, or paint like a sudden blanching. The woman stood there all in white, white dripping like liquid light, with a high white headdress (it would have to be a nylon wig), white bodice and streaked black and white skirt in which light was winning, and black shining high-heeled shoes. In the dead silence, a dead white face, utterly blank like an egg, the eyes and mouth screwed up, then the hand brushed across the eyes and the mouth, and the mouth opening, a red spot in the white, and laughter coming out, the shocked and silent decorators now falling about laughing, the painted lady of the house clutching her womb and laughing, all falling about laughing, laughing and pointing!

21

As Gregory Treviles walked up the platform to join the train that was to take him back to Cornwall, he glimpsed an elegantly red-bloused high-heeled figure just stepping into a carriage. Brid Hare was on the train! He was glad he had lagged behind that morning delayed by writing down his dreams; if he had encountered her leaving the hotel, or shared a taxi with her, he would out of politeness have had to sit with her in the train, and though now he might have to wave to her in the restaurant-car, bow slightly, and sit elsewhere, there'd be no six-hour flirting and mocking, which seemed to be her only mode of communication with the opposite sex. He wondered if it was any use talking to male patients like that, if one were a woman doctor.

As he sidestepped to avoid a large trolley of luggage, Treviles noticed that the privet hedge on the other side of the green-painted wooden paling still held a multitude of droplets from the morning shower. A sudden dizziness held him still as he looked into the forest of crystal fruit. He thought that he was held like a foetus in a great drop of clear water and the edges of his drop had touched one of the droplets that hung at the point of that leaf, there. It touched, and flowed, and gathered and dropped and he was falling past tier upon tier of green ledges on which people had gathered to watch him. He stopped. He stopped falling. He touched his forehead with his fingertips and found it bedewed with sweat. Steady again he found a carriage, fumbled with the catch, entered and sat down. He hoped nobody would join him; he spread his briefcase, coat and grip over the other seats so that they looked occupied.

The glitter from a puddle on the concrete platform held him. The sun shone in it and it looked solid, like a splash of gold. It was a Rembrandt gold helmet lying on the platform. A whistle blew, and he saw coloured feathers. The train lurched, and took the helmet away, slid it away slowly. Treviles knew that his studies had made him very susceptible to these hypnotic effects after a big and vivid dream. He also knew that he had done wrong by using the dream to taunt Al Bodkin, who had turned it back on him unwittingly, and now he was analysand, hypnotisee.

He took out a book. Now he was on guard. It was no lurid paperback but a book of poems. If it was a book of true poems, as he believed this one to be, then they would unite his powers and he could discover the truth in the fantasy. This poet was very fond of mildew, mould, decay, mud, dampness, which in his work were a kind of clearing-house for new growth, unformed life. The poems usually were about the transformation of what looked like sickness into new life and new powers. He read:

> Sit watching the mouldy wood,
> Bark peeling like old boots,
> Blazed with white fleece,
> Single-legged stools of pulp;
> It becomes to him, he says, a luminous interior,
> As though a dew-drop hoarded him,
> Rinsed cleaner eyes and gave him
> Light flowing at every damp point.
> Each spike of a leaf of every leafy tree,
> There, and elsewhere, scorched red by the season,
> Measures at him and beams in his direction,
> And where he is not he knows (he says)
> Other dewed forests receive and shine light
> In beds of light at every flashed tree-top,
> In every forest needles lacing in every direction,

And the quiet blazes there as it does for him here, (he
says).

'A synchronicity!' said Treviles aloud, 'a meaningful coincidence! My waters did not break. I was a droplet falling to the ground.' He re-opened the book at another page:

THE FLIGHT OF WHITE SHADOWS

Over the crooked notice-board crying 'Private',
Over 'Greenlease' one half rented to the weeds
That munch its shivering windows, over the wide flat waters
Streaked by the gulls with long white cries,
Tripling the reed-hiss, killing the reflections,
The brusque shower comes. Each drop binds in itself
A terrestrial globe for nobody's inspection
Incurving sky full of meadow, gravid horse, farm, folk
focused, each
Splashes itself many times over in leaves,
On rocks, worlds out of worlds, into worlds, before entering
The troubled horsetrough or the lying-down ditch
Still and long, that held a slightly vaster
Version of the sky. It is not a day for reflections,
Not even the smallest, of bird-bath, hoofprint, flowercup,
So slaughtered by swarming lives, the little bombs
Hacking away, whose twinkling self-assassinations
Tumble like consequences; confluences
Threading through tree-towers. A flap of thunder
Shakes out the clouds in the greatest of them all
Who, when in smooth vein, binds the sky into one salt,
One ferociously-curving whole whose theme is high sun
Boring his windy fire-holes — today is roof and ceiling,
Tiled and shattered snowing,
Racing acute edges on to the seashore.
Hordes strike, and forget themselves immediately, are gone
Water into water, or into stone speckling without sympathy,
So what afterlife for the vehemence of sheer-fall,
The blackener of the sky with the limpid on earth,

Spater, bridge-bungler, gouger of fellow-water,
Bruised eggs streaming with a thin vision,
Smashed fruit under black banners? The same, though
Drawn through rock, honeycombs of knives,
Staircases of razors, chasms of scimitars,
Sandy scythe-galleries, division and redivision,
Unlikely rejoinings, green amnesias — all
To the one reflection down river-paths,
Passed down by the rivers, down to that larger,
To the vastation, which is not
The same artist for an instant either.

'We never step twice into the same river; everything flows. All the molecules conscious, and crying to communicate. I was a single drop. All the people watching from emerald tier and terrace had risen up through the veins of the stems and the leaves. I never reached the ground, I could have risen too, or I might have become the watery body of a worm entering a graveyard, warehousings of human cheese, bound there for centuries. But this is a dream, I am not bound by dreams!' pronounced Treviles.

'Another poem.' Turning over the pages he glimpses the line: 'I lift my dews to what I shall become', but cannot again find the poem in which it occurred. Here was one:

Attend to the outer world.
See the calm delicate spray of the branches,
Watch the cool grey spurs of the sky
Sliding volumes the one over the other,
Listen, not inwardly to that gravel-crunch
(Yourself strolling over your nature,) but
Listen and wait, for,
Falling over the springy testing boughs,
The sliding volumes of the clouds and roads,
Out of the light clear rain shed,
Out of the open hot throat
The world attends you
Like a friendship, in three clear notes
Out of a bird's open throat.

Treviles looked up, out of the window. A bird, a swallow, was flying, keeping pace with the train, darting in and out its slipstream. He rose from his seat to get a better view and as he leant forward to the window he heard quite clearly the bird utter three clear notes as pure as pulses of spring water.

22

Three clear tones sounded in the room, and Robyn had a sudden and very clear picture of Gregory staring bolt-eyed through a window. 'Is he dead?' she wondered, and then 'what doors have I opened?' The reality of the three tones, like a bird's cry but also like the pulsing of a bell or a small gong was utterly real, and yet she also somehow knew that the source of the sounds was not in the room with her. She still got up to look, then she sat down again and made a note of the time on a pad. Next she went out to the telephone and rang the conference hotel. No, Dr Treviles had left by the morning train. There was nothing for her to do but fret. She had been bathing in the luxury of the white light conjured above her head, she had been, as it were, naked inside herself under the white waterfall of the imaginary flame that lived like pentecostal fire above the crown of her head. She had had many new thoughts, and even questions answered by this practice before now, but never before a direct hallucination or glimpse of what lay within and beyond the fire. Today it had been that waterfall, which she called the Force — this is the northern name, the Lake District name for a fall — at other times it had been a white flame, once it had become a little white figure of Jesus sitting on nothing in midair above her head small as a gnat or an enormous figure a million miles away and it was from his figure that the light streamed. Often her figure became rinsed clear like glass, and, having reduced the flame so its power was no longer operating, she would sit watching in her mind's eye her body cooling round the air it breathed, so that her lungs became visible first, like two complex seaweed-fronds spread in a pool, then the network of veins and arteries beginning with the major vessels and finishing with the swarms of capillaries that appeared like a pink mist through which she could see the massy bones sitting in their positions before the skin clouded the picture and finally her clothes appeared and she looked down at herself with closed eyes and to check her powers of visualisation made sure the picture was sharply in focus before she opened them to see that all coincided. The phone rang, then faltered and fell silent. She was standing by the front door remembering her white lights and considering her roses and wondering why the light above her head had never appeared in such a superb natural form, but always as something striving to split the grain of the air. Under the elm, its shadow, gnats even at mid-morning explored the grain of the air in their complicated dance that always made her think of a complicated greyhound-race run in three dimensions by hirsute dogs-Russian wolfhounds perhaps. Four dimensions? Often if you watched them a gnat appeared to wink out of existence. Had Gregory winked out of existence? It had not felt like that.

23

It was mid-morning. Gregory put down the book of poems called *The Force* and watched the green fields streaming past. He had never experienced the chiming of a poetry with actual happenings in quite that way before, though he had always believed it possible, and had treated patients in this way — by 'introjecting' some image of poetry into their waking minds so that it chimed with the development of a dream, so that it helped the dream unwind itself and thus altered the person's behaviour in the outer world. He had no doubt that persons before him had experienced visions from reading poetry, and that their minds had prophesied beforehand of the visions', they would receive. Indeed, he could see no other reason why poets should have been so revered in the ancient world if they did not have such power over the minds and bodies of people. What were the chants of shamans but poetry and practical therapy at one and the same time? And what was his therapy but trying to nudge the poems of the dreamer gently — or if necessary violently — into shape as the poet did his material, into shape, form, completion, a living growing thing. A large common of turf and furze began unrolling its recesses and paths past him. The train was travelling fast but he glimpsed at least seven hares chasing, jumping, rolling, boxing together in a dusty place by a green hillock. He had in that glimpse an intuition that they were following some pattern in the ground and within the grain of the air and as he watched one seemed to leap and vanish.

24

As she watched in the garden, wondering how to spend the time before meeting Gregory at the station, watching the gnats, a gnat seemed to wink into existence and join the others in their course and their jig. 'Am I dreaming again?' The creatures were so small it was easy to be deceived. There! it had vanished.

25

Magpies! such beautiful pied birds, large, graceful, and the ever-startling contrast of their black-and-white that had no trace of formality in it like penguins or even dalmatians, but made them like scarecrows in flight, rowing with their sleeves, or like the famous Romney Marsh smugglers who dressed as tattered ghosts on horses wearing black and white clothes to suggest skeleton mounts — these were powerful birds — and he had just seen a solitary magpie flying over a ploughed field towards the train: 'One for sorrow . . .' he would prefer a good omen. He blinked his eyes in surprise — a companion magpie had appeared by the side of the first. They must have been flying so close in formation that one of the pair had been invisible until that moment. They climbed and passed over the train. Treviles watched for their reappearance in the windows on the other side of the corridor, but they must have wheeled back. 'Two for joy . . .' Bird-hare. Brid.

26

Robyn was intrigued by two flecks of glitter on the hill-slopes to the north-west. From this distance it looked as though two fountains had been planted close together in the sun. She got the binoculars from the hallstand. Scarecrows! dressed in tattered black clothes pinned together with strips of silver foil that fluttered and clattered and played with the sunlight. She looked at them for a while, wondering why bird-scarers were needed on a hill of trees and grass, and which employee of the retired army officer who owned that hill had made this affectionate joke: two scarecrows in glittering garments standing hand in hand as for a gypsy wedding. Unlike the usual rustic courtship. She thought of the black hoop in her dream, and of the white-black dancers who tossed it over her head and made her disappear. She thought of the white hoop she tore open above her head for the uncreated light to pour down upon her. She looked for the scarecrows again and could not find them.

27

The fantasy, the dream must be followed through, to find whatever is real in it. Much play of the mind, much invention, stands against the knowledges that are new and real: it is as though these lurking powers that have always been in humanity press against an organ that has not yet been born, as one may see forms of light if one presses a finger against a closed eyelid. He had read the tragic story of Black Elk, the mighty Red Indian seer who had had a vision of his people's redemption under his tutelage, his magic tutelage subject always to the Grandfathers, the Powers of the World, and how he had been unable to live out his visions. Had he lived out his visions he would have rescued his people. Gregory thought that one must both beware of the 'Messiah complex', but not be afraid of it either. Every man in his own way must be taking part in the work of redemption, if it is to occur. Objects, animals had begun speaking to him in the way it was recorded they had spoken to the shamans, indeed to many discoverers in western society: to Strindberg, to Jung, to Pasteur, to benzene Kekulé, to Einstein. Objects were always speaking to the people we called mad. In his practice Gregory had learned to wait patiently for the inadvertent, underground remark, the mistake that revealed, the punning data, the stammer on the next to important word. If he, Gregory, was going mad from too much psychological practice, then he was so; he only prayed he did not fall into the hands of one of his 'sane' colleagues, like Dr Hare. He did not believe that he Gregory was anything more than a child of the educated English middle classes, a very commonplace phenomenon, something with a good brain and very, very innocent; but his chosen profession had taken him into darker places and now (perhaps by the grace of his patients' madness) he was growing up — which might to Dr Hare and her colleagues look like regression and a backsliding into common madness. But surely it was what all men through all cultures had in common — emotion, magic, play — that was important — hope, power, communion — it was only now that we made the new kind of man, or woman, the unplayful, the unmoved, the unpoetic, the well-paid, our masters.

The backward journey to his slate home with Robyn unreeled before Treviles as he made these cogitations to soothe asleep that part of him that was not to be the chief instrument of these travels. The analytical part of his intelligence as he watched the fields and houses flicker past, the countryside growing more and more rural as they penetrated further west, this part of him was alert for new hares, new disappearing birds, new 'phenomena' and this was not true alertness, but a defence — let me see it before it gets inside me. We shall need that later, he said to himself, but now I must give myself up to what comes as completely as if I were falling asleep but I will be both untroubled and awake.

Gregory thought in rains. They would not touch the ground so he thought in terms of rocks crowned with ice. He thought in terms of smaller stones since the great circles took so long, and he thought now of a scree that lifted in a whirlwind with a great screeching and built a mountain-cairn. The cairn surveyed the land. A climber approached with a new stone in his hand. Gregory thought in terms of hands that built bonfires, and with the aid of these hands he plucked the smokes of bonfires and carried them slowly oozing like great orangey-brown snails on his open palm, and like cornucopias that were dark as slate with ribbons of flame.

A hand shook his shoulder. He said 'Not now.' He looked into the cloudy blue eyes of the guard. 'Tickets please.' He closed his eyes after the man had gone.

Now he thought in terms of his next door neighbour, Mrs Louvain, singing as she stood by the garden gate. This was the last sound he heard as he lay dying on the slate bed in the upstairs bedroom. He was too weak to call Robyn back as he heard the swish of her starched skirts leaving the room. The red setter springs up the steps from the garden. It starts to yelp and whine in the hall but Robyn hushes it. A light rain begins to fall. Its fresh smell enters the room. Now it falls persistently, savagely. The wind gets up from its kneeling on the sea, howls through the deer-park, over the croquet lawn. Tall black clouds full of gates opening and closing on heavenly blue, race across the sky. Wind drives the water into the ground, into the sides of the hill. Dr Treviles takes a deep breath, and dissolves into it. Rain pelts down upon Robyn in their garden, she is crying, the rain mixes with her tears, her red hair and red dress cling to her, bright as fresh blood. Suddenly with a cry water streams upwards from the grass, Robyn disappears in a cloud of water pulling itself from the strands of her clothing and her hair rises as the water streams upwards into the clouds. The garden-pond empties itself into the sky and sails away like a glass gondola. Dr Treviles exhales and comes to himself. He opens his eyes on the flickering green scenery.

Earth would not accept water. Sky and land would not be brought together. Rain would not refresh the land. At what point did the vision reverse? At the sight of Robyn standing bright as fresh blood.

So he thought of blood, but he took it unawares. He thought of himself after death when he would become a furnace that had a particular skill: it could run the silver round the gold to assist the jeweller. Gold was blood of the sun. He would also after death be a red stool in Snow Hall. He thought of drugs, of those which in large quantities could be used for death, and in small quantities provided illumination. He thought of wolf-bane with its blue flowers, the aconite, and he ground it up with soot from the chimney, and baby-fat from the iron pot. He thought of the wolves that caught the baby, and of the trampled bloody snow.

The howling of wolves put him in a coach rattling along behind four bolt-eyed black-plumed horses in Transylvania. Not for a thousand gold gourds would the coachman stay behind in these woods after dark. He alighted from the coach with his black leather grip containing sharp stakes and an iron-headed mallet and three Bodkin-blessed rosaries with crucifix. A blue mist made three white shapes of women through the trees. He set off through them with a firm step. Now he made offering in the ruined chapel. He had trained himself to draw blood from the vein in the crook of his arm. The blood is in the chalice, he makes the invocation, a faint blue steam rises from the warm blood in the cold air.

Nema! Live morf su reviled tub . . .

A tension gathers across the blood-surface, and the chalice grows too heavy to hold up. Knowing the sign, he pulls the bowl of blood like a hoop slowly downwards off the cloaked shadow. The blood bowl rests on the bare earth. The shadow suddenly wheels, presses something into Gregory's hand, turns a face to him that is bolt-eyed, nostrils flared and fangs dribbling blood, and runs from the chapel overturning the blood-bowl. Blood sinks into the ground, hissing, in snaky coils.

On his knees, Gregory looked at the Satan's Stone Dracula had left in his hand as he ran out to join his three misty sisters in the wood.

Gregory held Satan's Stone in his hand. This was the name an Edwardian wanderer had given to a certain red pebble found on the slopes of a Japanese volcano. These strange pebbles are caused by an accidental splash-formation of the lava. They come in any size but of one invariant shape on which can easily be seen the pattern of a narrow chin and broad forehead, and on the brow two small excrescences shaped like unopened rosebuds or minute wings. From the first time they were seen in the village market-stalls it was quite clear that they were lucky stones. As charms, they resemble to some the head of a demon, and are therefore effective in keeping off such demons, since if a demon encounters the severed head of a fellow-member of his legions, he will fly. Others take them as fortunate natural representations of a human or animal womb with the *ligamenta lata* sometimes called 'the vase of sins', and as an emblem of fertility and prosperity they make good sales to young married women and farmers. Gregory saw them displayed in heaps on a stall in a small market village near Koshiro. Running his thumb over the oddly attractive excrescences, it struck him with no little force that it was not only in the backward places of the world that good-luck emblems were prized. And these were good quality pumice stones ready shaped so that if they caught on in the perfumed bathrooms of the West two closely-related lusts, those of cleanliness and superstition, were at once satisfied to his great profit.

Gregory at once rented the lava fields which were no less a loose scree of Satan Stones, most of a handy size, some attaining the size of Easter Island statues, but thrown all higgledy. His men soon arrived on the scene shipping them off in lorry-loads. He lost no time in hiring an advertising agency that offered him two separate campaigns: A/B income group 'Bathe in the sinful luxury of Satan's Stone' and C/D group 'Lusty bathtimes with the Vase of Sins'. There was also 'Lucky Bathtimes with Jimmy Pisky' for the children. The adult versions were illustrated with couples embracing in a great womb-shaped bath among much copulatory foam. Treviles O.K.'d these, but also asked them to work on a reserve treatment for the more hygienic journals of 'Brace your skin with Satan's Stone'. This in the event proved the most popular of all the advertisements, for the rubbing of town-grimed skins with the fine pumice produced a healthy tingle, indeed a feeling of well-being in the skin that resembled a post-coital flush. In no time at all people despised those who did not by their flesh appear to have risen recently from a bed of love, and the fashion was not only comfortable but became obsessively popular. The rag trade benefited very much, for fine and closely-woven garments were a necessity to the sensitised skins of populations of men and women who now possessed, as Treviles's enthusiastic advertising agency now called it in a follow-up barrage of advertisements, 'Satan's Satin Skin'; and lotions of all kinds that pampered this new organ of sensation thrived. Treviles was gratified to present at his own expense an Easter Island sized Satan's Stone to the Hampstead Borough Council for subaqueous installation in their new children's swimming and Turkish Bath centre, where it loomed under the lighted water like a a statue of Moloch.

The first sign of a breakthrough came one morning when Treviles opened his *Times* to see unusually large headlines proclaiming how Lord Excrate, one of the richest men in England — who had recently been blinded by a shower of sparks from a blast-furnace belonging to a steel firm he was inspecting with a view to closure — had arisen in wrath from his bath-tub, where he had been rubbing his Satan's Stone meditatively over his poor sightless forehead because he liked the feeling, and had fought and overcome with the skills of perfect vision certain burglars who were after his cloisonné. (One of these turned out to be a titled rival collector whose injuries put him in hospital for half a year.)

Such perfect vision streaming from glaring red empty sockets (for his Lordship had removed his glass eyes for his bath, placing them in the soap dish) had panicked the burglars — the one who had not been caught by Lord Excrate embraced the constable who arrived in answer to the burglar alarm and demanded police protection. Later medical examination proved (said *The Times* medical correspondent) that the forehead of the rich blind man was awake with a panoramic vision that far exceeded the capacities of the organs that he had lost. In a cyclorama-like strip which was also three-dimensional (rather than stereoscopic like the normal eye) he perceived the radiations not only of light but of heat also. These appeared to penetrate and stand in the new sensoria like a coherent light hologram, since the possessor of this sense perceived objects in a manner which enabled him also to see round these objects without himself moving. Long magnetic waves (further tests showed) were also perceived like dark shadows cresting slowly through the walls of a room, and short radio waves were weakly visible like a wavering and constant light of an unknown colour falling everywhere.

It soon became apparent that Lord Excrate was not alone in the possession of these faculties. Dermo-optical perception (as it was called) quickly became a commonplace — some small shock was needed to open the skin to sight after Satan's Stone had been in use for a few days, and many people claimed the perception of moral qualities through the examination of the auras of others.

Before any government could intervene, the examination of auras became a skill accessible to the great mass of people. Life became superbly worth living once more for people deprived of luxuries — the great majority — who could not understand where the radiant perceptions of their childhood had escaped to. The governments themselves, those that gave more than a show of democracy, rapidly improved, for no man can convince from the hustings when he is surrounded with a visible odour the colour of rotten apples burning with a smoky flame that stinks to high heaven of insincerity.

Nations united to make weather control a practical possibility at first by means of warm climatodromes that enabled their inhabitants to remove all clothing twenty-four hours a day, since garments impeded the vision of the skin. Skin showed its transformations by the rainbow colours racing over it or held steady in visible consideration and development by the adept watching his own body, reflection in the true sense. Later the climatodromes were abandoned when it was found that quite small batteries of persons sitting back to back and concentrating in a certain manner could 'hypnotise the weather' — over a wide area — every citizen was expected to perform in this manner for a few hours in a year, like jury service. A new contemplative religion was born. There were to begin with frequent mob panics when the new perceptions proved too vivid and rich for many people reared on television. There were also reports of 'ghosts'. One horrible report told of a family of six, husband, wife and four children ranging from sixteen to four, who were found hanged in a reputedly haunted house, all swinging from the same beam in a locked and bolted attic. It was thought that what they had seen and had driven them to the upper storey, and what awaited them on the stairs, had proved too much for them to bear. The new religion proclaimed that these 'ghosts' were entirely natural, and that by mild flagellation and the frequent application to the skin also of Satan's Stone in an atmosphere of earnest prayer, the whole time of a given place could be held as a standing wave in the skin of a single individual: he then contemplated the mutations of time and fortune in a single moment, like God, *sub specie aeternitatis*.

However, the first person to step out of his skin was not a member of this contemplative order, but that same eyeless millionaire who had routed his housebreakers with glaring red sockets and impossibly accurate blows from an iron poker. He translated himself in full view of his household staff one Sunday lunchtime. He had forked a piece of roast beef to his mouth, chewed it, swallowed it, taken a sip of red wine, dabbed his lips with his napkin, said 'excuse me' to nobody in particular since he was lunching alone, naked, of course, pushed back his chair and walked to the large mirror on the wall. He stood there for a moment, gave a long sigh, and crumpled to the floor. The butler stepped forward, then stopped. Still standing in front of the mirror was a figure resembling his master but apparently made of rainbow patterns that shifted oilily. The test match commentary on the small portable radio set that always stood by his Lordship's place at table was interrupted by a crackle of static and a squawk of parrots, and then by a majestic voice at an immense volume that told the butler that he was not to touch the figure (it said 'noli me tangere' but translated it immediately when the man did not appear to understand), since his Lordship had converted himself to a body of resonating electromagnetic waves: having taught himself to do so by studying the patterns of radiation that he had been receiving through his skin. Having spoken through the radio set, the butterfly-man walked straight through the oak panelling. Rushing to his master's fallen body, the butler found that it was indeed an empty and uninhabited carcass.

Lord Excrate was but the first of many to step out of their skin. The populations of the world became one vast rainbow pattern of radiation pulsing over the entire globe in a song of great joy and reality. Should an individual need to reacquire his material envelope, then it was a simple matter to slow down the vibration of part of the broadcast he had become, and walk about on two legs again, among as many material objects as he needed and which he could obtain by means of a similar precipitation, with the greatest of ease. The commonest shape adopted by those whose need it was to travel in waking dream to the farthest places of the universe (whose corners contained wonders that the unprepared mind could not comprehend and certainly not travel to in its own mode, despite its composition of radiation and its superb capacity for modulating), was that of the Satan Stone. In due time all of humanity toured the wonders of the universe, penetrating fastnesses of incredible peril, environments of impossible kinds, the interiors of stars, the inside-out universes of the 'black holes', while keeping their basic personality-modulation by means of the Satan Soulstone shape. The devil headstones were arranged in their millions in great rows on high places and the whole earth resembled Easter Island with its wise heads who had achieved this before the remainder of humanity (and this is the explanation of Easter Island). In two places at once, winging among the stars, regarding the stars from their living cemeteries of Satan Headstones, humanity shaped itself in compliment to the demon-form that had fulfilled Blake's prophecy in 'The Marriage of Heaven and Hell', spoken by one of his devils of energy, that 'The Kingdom of Heaven on Earth will come by an improvement of Sensual Enjoyment.'

Robyn sat turning over the great shiny pages of a coffee-table book, Brancusi . . . Easter Island . . .

The train stopped at Plymouth Station. A great noise of doors and people. Gregory resisted the temptation to open his eyes, and immediately found himself inside a television set. The cathode tube, he saw, was womb-shaped, with the fundus (on which coloured pictures were projected) pointing out into the room and the vestibule packed with electrodes like so many penises projecting visions into the womanly organ. He looked about him at the small shelves of transistors like a neat library, or a coloured garden of electrical scaffolding, and perceived that the basic pattern of the whole thing was also yoni-lingam since straight currents everywhere were modulating circular ones that travelled in coils. At this he realised that the set was turned on and that he was caught up in a great hot orgy of electricity. Turning about to find some escape, he put his hand on a wire and with a green flash along all his nerves was pulled in among the jockeying currents. 'The State of the Party' said an announcer solemnly, and Gregory found himself holding a martini-glass and looming over an excitable Alec Bodkin, who was twittering at him. A hovering female hand beyond the glass great as an acres-flock of swallows adjusted the tone control. 'I've been running a newspaper, Gregory. You should try it.'

Gregory eyed his friend's rusty black and his Aguecheek hair. 'It's a new thing. Totally. I print only the events that happen in the night. Nothing daytime. All the news that's fit to print between sunset and dawn. Robberies, child-murders (including the use of condoms and other barriers)', continued the electrical wraith of the Christian priest, as the distant camera swung round for close-ups of his babbling lips and the tilted martini-glass, 'a section recounting the dreams of world-leaders telexed as they happened from bugged pillows with swansdown antennae. The arts-pages review night-written books, as so many of them are, but ignore the fresh and rational pages that occur when the sun is up. Personal columns detail the minutiae: who intends doing what with whom and how during the hours of darkness.' Gregory noticed that his god-collar had a little metal tab on it stating: 'Alexander Chesney Bodkin, M.A., B.D., 1932–' and the latter date was engraved but he twitched his head before Gregory could read it. 'Furthermore we do not spare to carry in our agony columns such cris de coeur as: Teddy: I shall wank at 11.03 precisely. With you in spirit. In our advertisement columns you will find who intends to smoke what, drop what, pop what, long lists of assassins offering their services, all-night chemists, and large illustrated coverage of night-beverages, bedclothes, night-garments, penis-rings, dildoes, arc-lamps, infra-red snipers' gear, hypnotism-mirrors revolving by clockwork, dream-books, witches' cradles and other equipment for astral travel including the latest most sophisticated sensory deprivation kit, star-maps and quarter-scale models of Stonehenge in heavy plastic for making lunar observations on one's own front lawn.'

'Does the paper sell? Does it make money?' asked Treviles languidly.

'My biggest scoop was the Moon Murders. I was the first to publish the nightside disclosures of that business. I sold the tapes of the children's seduction, rape and murder. I made a best-selling record of them. It was in the top twenty. It was a golden disc. I tell you Treviles, these tapes did for baby-sacrifice what colour printing did for Da Vinci . . .'

'You ought to be ashamed, Alec,' said Gregory weakly.

'I am ashamed my dear, but I know how to weep for horror. Do you know how to weep for horror?'

Two great stones rolled out of Alexander's eyes and dropped on the carpet. A passing dowager watery with diamonds stepped in one of them. Her foot slewed forward and the portly performed a slithering pratfall full-length along the brown slide and fetched up against the punch-bowl table which slowly collapsed hot and flaming on her head. Screaming, hair ablaze, she ran out of the room to the howling laughter of the studio audience. Final take of Bodkin, reading his office out of a little black book which by the inverted gold cross on the cover was upside-down, looks slyly up, waggles eyebrows, roll credits.

Robyn looked up from her book of Leonardo drawings. Was that a car at the gate? She heard the catch ring as it closed and hurried footsteps coming up the path. Alex Bodkin came into view. He waved at her. They met at the front door. 'Is Gregory back?' 'No, Robyn, he was on the train. I came to ask whether you wanted a red setter puppy. It's a really rich auburn with lighter-coloured ears. I heard you wanted a dog.' Robyn turned away for a moment. She had looked at this man's face. There was not a trace of guilt or guile in it. He was about Gregory's age, but he looked much younger. She supposed his religion kept him young, in this parish anyway.

Gregory felt he must find his way out of the party, which looked like going on after the performance. He walked round the side of the painted studio flat of the party-room and bumped into the stout burned lady who had taken her wig off revealing a man's short hair, she was wiping the cold cream off her face, off his face. Gregory smelt fresh air. An iron door led out of the great studio shed. As he opened it, he looked back. The stage ended in a great curving glass screen through which he could only see blurred shapes. A flickering hand great as a flock of sparrows approached and descended. An intuition took Gregory swiftly out of the door. There was a loud click like the chonk of an axe and the whole doorway went milky and hard, like a glass marble or a dead fish's eye. He closed the iron door on that dead world.

As he walked home — but where was home? — the solid moonbeams like misty roots littered the path. The stars were arranged in depth, like a thorn-bush of electricity. He would not open his eyes, he saw with closed eyes, he would not open his eyes to the Moon Murders, the Rich Pig Murders, the Hitler Murders — who then was he to live in the world, practising psychology, ignoring such things. He had never in his practice met a murderer. I ought to do a stint at Broadmoor. He felt like a child to Bodkin whose heart was full of *The Jesus Murder*. But these murders were outside him in the world. Then they were also inside him, and if he went mad, then he might kill, he might elect a sacrifice and eat its heart. He remembered a dream he had read about — just the words came to him now, no explanation, no interpretation, no canny snatching at the important part to give it back to the dreamer, just the words: 'The hare looked up at me with trusting eyes. I had to cut into its fur. The hare looked trustingly at me as I cut into it, and my knife slipped into the haunch.' As Gregory walked home, the hare looked at him with trusting eyes. Dr Treviles carried his large scalpel, and his bone-saw. There was a funeral arranged. His coming was announced. The ants were at stretch, the stars were at stretch, the hares were at stretch and here he came with his bonesaw and plastic sheet to gather up the blood. He passed the churchyard and appreciated with the eyes of one intimate with the dissecting room the horrible odours of colour, the disgusting blorts of smashed flesh that clung to the bones of his patients that he had signed off for the last time. Graveclothes sopping with cheesy varnish, face disappeared in bilberry and custard through which, wiping off with a clownish grave-cloth, the shining bones appeared. The masks that came off during the wake! The expressions that unreeled (as my journey in this train unreels scenes I have known for so many years; and his eyelids trembled in their moisture): the whole career of faces, and some stopped at middle age and some were as cheeky with their dead smiles as schoolboys and some were as peaceful as if they had been born again and some had the waxy heavy-lidded omniscient look of the foetus. And they went into their boxes and decayed like smashed pastries and if you could see the smell, what a rainbow!

He left the churchyard gate and began to mount Fentonluna Lane. His coming was announced. At the little well that was set in the deerpark wall halfway up, he felt ill again. Gregory knelt on the wet grass and vomited up what looked like a custard pie, sloppy but firm, clingy. Custard for brunettes, he thought; bilberry for blondes. He levered himself to his feet, and transferring the bone-saw to his left hand, splashed water on his face with the right. At the front door he paused, then knocked with great blows three times. Robyn opened the door and he raised his scalpel. She switched on the overhead light. She was naked, but her vulva was a great mass of blood that dripped. Treviles raised his scalpel high and plunged it in a glittering arc straight into his own heart. Robyn smiled, and shut the door. After a pause, the overhead light went out.

Treviles has dropped his bone-saw and he attempts, once more on his knees, to enlarge the wound the scalpel has made, for he must have missed the heart. There is sticky wetness everywhere that he cannot see, but there is no pain. He might have been attacked by a bilberry pie fiend, for all the pain there is. Though there is a light somewhere far off and away, that might be a pain if it came closer.

Robyn wanted to say to Alex that she had misjudged him. At the same time, if she admitted that she had done so, that in itself would express rancour that she had no intention of communicating. So she decided to remain silent. 'The dog?' said Alex again eagerly. Three resounding thumps came echoing through the house from the back door, in Fentonluna Lane. With a wail Robyn ran through the house and opened the door and stood staring up and down the lane. To her left she saw one of the stags had pushed open the gate. It stared at her and wheeled back into the park. The stag wouldn't charge her back door! Besides, she saw it nudging the gate. 'Alec, it's no one. But would you shut the Colonel's gate?'

There is a pain some way off and it is coming closer. It is also a light containing trees. A voice says 'You invited me with fire and pain. Now by main force you have drawn me here.' The three solitary oaks in the Frome meadow multiply and the forest is made of many grand trees. Rain falls between the fretted leaves, between the exquisitely polished acorns. Through the corridors of trees I see movements, flashes, swiftnesses. Some are russet brown, and some are pink-white. It is getting dark, night is falling. The smoky rain ceases. I come to a dell of dry leaves beneath the oldest trees. There are mossy stumps resting in the dry leaves.

By a mossy stump I see an intertwined heap of brown skin and white limbs. The heap moves richly. I hear inviting sounds, deafening sighs. I tread on a twig, and the sound announces me like a dry bell. The brown pelt disentangles itself from the white limbs, and God rises to his feet. He is curly-headed and bends over his woman, who is sleeping; then he turns his head which carries the fine seven-tined antlers towards me, and smiles with his strong and kindly face.

He walks towards me, a strong athlete's walk.

He is much taller than I am, six and a half feet perhaps, plus the antlers, which add another two or maybe three feet.

He comes closer to me. I drop my camera.

I wonder if his antlers ever catch in the lower boughs of the trees, and I wonder if he is ever hunted, and who hunts him. He bends and kisses me on the lips. It is being kissed by warm bark and plumage, and the smell is strong, rich and useful, like fresh-sawn wood.

Then another sound catches his attention and he stiffens, staring behind me, over my shoulder and into the trees at the edge of the forest, the direction from which I came. Then I hear the yelping of hounds — I have led them to him!

I saw God under sentence of death, I saw his hounds streaming like fire through the trees. I saw his pain-dance in ropes of blood he danced to untie.

The blood hoop, the fire hoop, the great whirlpool of the world, I take the baby's head and ease it out of the blood hoop and I whack its buttocks and it blushes all over and begins to yell, announcing his coming.

Which forest will he now not part like curtains? Which cliff-face, which tide? Is there a place I shall not see him, is there a place to hide?

In whose boot-cupboard would he be found? From whose larder would he step forth?

A sudden murmur from behind the closed doors of the street:

The doors of the street fly open and all the men and women and children of the street step back through their doors, ushering into the open air one man.

The one man leaves them, he strides off along the highway towards the city. His antlers are wreathed with vines. Behind him, the table-tops and chattels of the householders shimmer with electricity. The householders shimmer with electricity.

It began with only a few people — one or two in every thousand, but always thirteen in every million — performing his actions and rites, secretly, keeping his festivals. A liturgy grows, one passes among them preaching a single lesson from the great German's Faust-book: that Faust raised the spirit they sought and turned him away.

SPIRIT. 'Who calls upon me?'
FAUST: 'Oh terrible to see!'
SPIRIT: You feed upon my works, with strength
You call on me, and now—'
FAUST: 'Appalling vision!'
SPIRIT: 'Cannot endure the truth.'

So that Goethe's book ended almost before it began; in fact continued in a sterile debate with a bantering intellectual who Faust could never now shake off until he stepped out of his skin to the sound of a heavenly chorus, and Mephistopheles retired under a barrage of blood-red flowers, the heavenly monthly roses. This apostle writes letters which have wide currency and preach absolute secrecy.

Now every family performs these rites, in absolute secrecy, separately, in their own homes, and when he comes he comes into all these homes at one and the same time.

And one day he came, pouting and farting and trampling; bestowing electricity, rheoscopy and understanding. Gregory wipes the vomit off his lips, he looks down at himself for the wound but it is gone, though his shirt over his heart is cut cleanly without bloodstains as with a razor. And his heart throbs with a pain which looks like a hoop of light in which he can see trees.

The man jumps through the bonfires and lifts up the smoke of the bonfires and carries them on the palms of his hands. He scries with them, and offers you scrying. In the flooding smoke there are all the seasons of earth and air; in the church procession he carries them like slowly dance-writhing idols, tall grey totem countenances, sad, high and working. They utter responses and give commandments from long grey beards drawing down their woolly brows and when they have thundered enough he claps his hands together and cancels them with a joyful and easy gesture, rubbing off the little greasy marks Jehovah's smoke has left on the pelt of his thighs.

Then he sings with an infamous voice, like Le Petomane hands on knees and head over shoulder with the gases of his strong gut, and a boy-acolyte comes forward with a taper and lights this song which burns with a high thin voice that is blue and electrical; and he pinches off that flame and it floats down the nave to the head of the red setter lying quietly by the font, and the setter stands and begins to sing with the flame standing tall and lambent on the crown of its head; and then in turn he pinches flames off which are relighted each time by the boy-acolyte until the whole congregation is singing sweetly with the flames at the crowns of their heads. Lastly he serves his acolyte and himself with these flames but his own last flame stands between his antlers and all are singing with words that prophesy and they leave the church in procession and flames from the procession breed flames that float upon the heads of all the children, and the robins, and the magpies and the scarecrows, and the apple-tree is alight with the Elmo's fire, each fruit a voice, and the grasses and the wasps and the bees and the swans on the lake and the man in the tractor and the tractor and the gravestones each has a flame on it and then the flames enter the grave soil and the dead rise and join the living congregation in their singing.

Alex bought Robyn a platform ticket. They went through the barrier. Alex looked at his watch. Robyn pointed to a puff of steam that was drifting towards them through the plantation of young saplings. Then the train came puffing round the bend and drew in with a discord of metal brakes gripping hot wheels. The windows slid past them as the train came to a halt. Robyn looked through the pane that had stopped opposite her and straight into Gregory's staring eyes and gasping mouth. She made a quick gesture of comfort and looked to right and left for a door, but not before she had seen that the reflection of tree-branches on the glass gave Gregory the appearance of great antlers fastened to his head. A door opened a little way up the train. Down stepped Brid Hare neat in her red blouse and carrying a small square case. Their glances swept across each other but did not meet. She was quickly forgotten as Robyn pushed her way into the train.

END OF PART ONE

Part Two

Robyn and Brid to Gregory

I

'Are you a Mason?'

'You know I'm not.'

'A Rosicrucian?'

'Never met one.'

'Your father was a Mason.'

'Yes.'

'I bet he could build a tower better than you, otherwise you'd not be here.'

'Bitch!'

'Here it comes.'

'Rose-croix bitch!'

'That's better. Now let me . . .'

'Blood-bath! Countess Dracula!'

'It's good for you. Hormones. Make you grow.'

And astride him she leant back sliding her hips with a full look about her closed eyelids and red hair quiet in the darkened bedroom. Her lips went tight and her cheeks drawn for a moment, then she relaxed and looked down at him.

'That's twice.'

'I'm good at it.'

'Come on your side.'

'Yes.'

Afterwards he was silent inside. His head said nothing to him, he listened for things that it might say, but it was empty as a great attic above an empty calm house. 'Robyn . . .'

'Yes?'

'When I came in that first time, I was walking by the river with you. Where the willows are.'

'So was I.'

'But when I came my once to your how many? When we were sideways . . .'

'That was beautiful . . .'

'I saw a strange thing. You know the light you get on your lids when an eye gets knocked, stars, seeing stars? That happened to me when we came.'

'Did you see stars?'

'No, I saw — an amphora. A graceful slim vase with handles.'

'I know what you saw. Me.'

'That's sweet. But what?'

'You had a womb-flash, my darling.'

2

Robyn was out arranging wheat and fruit for the harvest festival. Treviles watched television. The programme was about life and death on the savanna. How the grass burned every Spring, and how the fertile plains thrived on this burning. Gregory took notes, balancing the shiny black notebook on his knee.

He watched the sweet resigned faces of gazelles, slaughtered meat of the lions, he watched the business-like pecking order of the various grades of vulture, and how they all waited for the large species of vulture to arrive, that which had the great beak that alone could pierce the hide of the prey.

What was the instinct to submit, and close your eyes willingly in death? Gregory had tasted it. What was the instinct to slaughter, and look into the eyes that were closing with submission? Gregory had tasted this. There was something beyond what he had delved into, something beyond slaughterer and slaughtered, that had to do with sexual joy. Robyn lowered herself on him, bleeding like meat. He had seen when she came, like a blow to the eye, the seal or stamp of her womb — this was one of those kind of events that did not taste of fantasy, but had stepped outside fantasy — though it had happened through love play. Truly women were powerful at this time — Robyn came with him on her seventh orgasm. His love had learnt stamina, but he was no longer able to produce more than two ejaculations, sometimes a little extra ghost-one that she gave him. And yet, she said (glowing in her hollow wand, and always dreaming of red tulips) his penis reverberated, always, with her. So the sensations that he had, which were sometimes exquisite ticklings, sometimes visions, 'trips', all came from down there, the rosy waves that rolled over his belly and chest, the sudden pictures of them together, until the moment when he completely joined her down below and came finally!

It is all as the animals expect: it is as if the hardly dead meat streaming with juices rested for a moment on the tongues of its predators and there mixed sweetly with the juice of the digestion, as though the meat tasted the eater, with joy.

In bed at last, the house empty around him, he dozed and watched rapid vivacious pictures of lions giving birth to gazelles and antelopes. He felt the garden child come in from the pond and get into bed with him, and he felt its thin cold arms clasp his back and he fell asleep.

Robyn, returning, closed the front door behind her, gently. 'I . . . love. The sun . . . is shining . . . Love' singing about the afternoon in bed with Gregory.

3

A child who is a genius, thrown into a trance by almost any occurrence. This is my theme. His soul dives deep into his body and enters another's body, any person or object. X-Ray diffraction plates look like holograms, I have seen crystal diffraction pictures of DNA. Its spiral code in the genes grows us. Why, I think it is a three-dimensional hologram, that grows us in height, stoutness, width and in the fourth dimension of time - could an instantaneous man exist? Of what body is it a hologram? What is also imaged by a double spiral? The sun and the moon. And the mitochondria for planets.

Might Endenberg like these ideas?

I mean that the sun and the moon run in their orbits like a double spiral, and the nucleoprotein has taken a three-D photo of this, Professor Carstairs, and we are a middle-scale reproduction of this photo.

Do you mean to say, Miss Treviles, that the sun and the moon walk about on the surface of the earth as men and women? Certainly. Is that not a trifle far-fetched? All great discoveries are, Professor Carstairs. But this is not a discovery, Miss Treviles. It is an opinion. Such correspondences, Professor, cannot be meaningless. If you allow the pulse-beat of a man to be his instant of time, and you give him a life of eighty-four years, the corresponding instant of time for the solar system is eighty-three years. Can you show this by calculations? Certainly Professor (rummaging in her briefcase) they are here. To continue, looking at the Solar System like this is to see a man made up of radiation and other electromagnetic effects, each part modulating every other part, a rainbow of a man, a rainbow man of flame, a man of vibration and harmony; and each of the planets orbits within him at the exact level of an endocrine gland. And what is this man doing, Miss Treviles? He is flying in a spiral from Sagittarius out towards Gemini, Professor.

Dr Endenberg scribbles on a piece of paper which he slides across to Carstairs. The latter nods, says: Miss Treviles, we like patterns here at An Cuntellow, and we like details. Dr Endenberg is interested in your patterns of ideas, so we shall second you to his seminar at Tintagel College. As for ourselves, we shall prefer to make use of your laboratory expertise here at Ruan Minor, where I should prefer you to confine yourself to showing students how not to break the apparatus (he laughed here to show that he was joking, really; his chin was like a small hard golf ball) and let the cosmos in. Have you transport . . . ?

'One of the first things I'll do at that lab is to test the holy well water for natural LSD' thought Robyn as she left the metal and white plastic seminar room after her interview. Now all the people had got into her head, and she had replayed the scenario several times. It was a *sign* of her excitement. 'I don't mind them getting into my head!' She stopped and looked for a moment at the façade of Ruan Manor, now part of the Department of Chemistry and Molecular Biology. She plucked an ivy leaf and rubbed the stalk in her fingers, and smelt the pungent juice, '. . . so long as they aren't phoneys after all,' she said.

4

Robyn and Gregory approached the holy well by way of the clay ravine, helping each other across the muddy path. As the ravine narrowed, the clay was replaced by flat grey-black slates arranged in packed strata.

The musty smell of the water seeping from the neglected garden above and up from the well-spring reminded Gregory of the smell of ivy-sap. It stood on the path — one moment fresh and the next water-musty — like a swinging door that was closed until they pushed against it and passed within.

The well-head was another door in the lichened wall, rather squat and narrow and dark. A leering face poked out of the lintel: as they came closer they saw that the leer was made of three compassionate bearded faces, looking one to the left, one to the right, and the third straight at them.

Robyn hung back from the well, staring at the tricephalon above it. Her boots leaked.

Inside the dark little sentry-box of stone, the clear water of the well lay like a tarnished glass tile set in the floor. He could just get his shoulders in, and they darkened the surface further as he stared into it. At first he could not understand the reflection he saw shadowed in the water. It goggled and leered and wobbled and he realised that he was interpreting the shadows as though he were still looking at the triple head that guarded the water-shrine. As his eyes comprehended these shadows, as they gradually rested from the tremor of his entrance, like the libration of a balance-needle, he could see that his face was dark. It was as if he were looking out of darkness, with darkness, into the darkness of his face. The darkness of the shadow seemed to go a long way down into the well. The entry however lighted his hair from behind, and the colour of this appeared in the water like a webwork of forces surrounding the black disc, like a solar corona at an eclipse, when the moon passes between the earth and the sun. He dipped a finger in the well and touched it to his forehead, just above the place where the frowns came. It was burningly cool. His finger surprisingly had hardly disturbed the water, the reflection was almost independent of the three ripples it made, the one at entering, the one as the finger left the surface again, and a third pulse across the mirror as a droplet of dank water fell back from his fingertip into the spring. He heaved himself up from his knees and turned to face Robyn. He was so conscious of the cool patch on his brow that he felt like a gigantic Cyclops rising out of the ground, but he doubted if the small dampness were visible.

'What was it like in there?' still looking above Gregory's head, examining the tricephalon.

'Timeless and musty, like lying in my coffin.'

Next time I'll open my eyes under that water . . . he watched Robyn kneel by the well. She took a small bottle from her pocket, filled it with water, replaced it. She remained with her head inside the stone well for a while. 'What did you see?' She shook her head. They both looked for a long moment at the lintel tricephalon again, turned, and went hand in hand back along the muddy ravine towards the brighter air.

5

Since dawn Robyn has been walking the rim of the cluster of valleys and she has seen and counted six separate tributaries of the river Reel, most of them fast brooks in water-meadow or woodland, and one a mere trickle through a silted re-entrant that became scree as she walked to the source: she found the tributary a fountain, wild and wise.

Her hair is very red; her head is full of the colours of water, the aftertaste of summer rain. Her heart is pounding as she climbs the hill called the Mump, which should give a seaward view of Petroc.

On the Mump's crest stand a group of oak trees forming a rough circle. Their dark shadows impound the sunlight. Stillness stands tall on each leaf. The atmosphere of the trees on the hilltop is of an ancient conversation which Robyn is interrupting. She pauses before entering the doorless doorway.

Inside the grove, her hair blazes in the green light, which is like the green of a perfect girl's wedding-dress. She is a sea-bride. The green water does not drown such as she. She is the red girl in the grove. She paces ceremoniously through the twenty-eight trunks passing them all taking a spiral path with the sun, clockwise, deosil until she reaches the little clearing at the centre. The turf here is thick and cool. She lies down — on an impulse she unbuttons her green blouse and removes it. She lets the oak-patterned sunlight wander through the skin of her breasts, through the nipples that are like eyes opened to the spiral day.

She falls asleep, whispering, 'Robyn, Robyn', to the leaves and knowing that there will be a seventh source on the other side of this hill — small conical hills like barrows always spring water at their foot. It is a very brief sleep, for the hot sun has moved hardly at all, but it was very full of children and talking dogs. There was a child scarcely out of nappies teaching a puppy to shit tidily on a flower bed by doing the same thing herself, showing the dog how. There was another, older, child, tossing a red setter wads of bloodstained cottonwool to eat. What sophisticated dreams! So many dreams were scarcely comprehended by the grown-up person; they were formed of the memories of when one rode inside one's mother like a submarine, or when you were two feet long and the same both ends with a skin like exterior cunt.

Reluctantly, Robyn dressed. A large insect bite glowed at the foot of her left Mump. Now she unwound her sunpath, widdershins between the crocodilian oaks.

True to her guess, a marshy spring bubbled from out of the Mump's foot, in a tangled copse of dwarf alders. Watch for vipers! With adroit clambering over tussocks of grass, she contrived to bend over the source where it rose in pulses within a narrow deep pool, and sip some of the water from her cupped palm, for the seventh time that day. The spring unwound from the marsh and pointed a way down the valley through green water-meadows, sung a way glittering and gurgling. The smell and taste and air feeling of all the tributaries she had partaken of today were each and every one different; she had felt chalk in the air and tasted it in the water; peat at another source; the granite stream had been steely and smooth; one had seemed the gutter of the world where people had thrown tins and plastic bags — a sheet of corrugated iron used as a cross between a bridge and a raft had discovered for her the unpolluted origin of this sad spot; the fifth plunged straight out of a cliff through an iron pipe set in a concrete panel; the sixth was green-mantled and full of tadpoles; this, the seventh, communicated alder and oak and the damp fissured barks of the trees it grew along itself. She went over each tributary in her mind; again she smelt the different locations of the water; again her eyelashes were cooled by the many breezes of the energetic water-shrines. Again she started off down a new valley, between new water-meadows.

The brook meandered, and gained force. The ground grew rockier. Great boulders sat in ferns, and deep within small woods. The flowing water had encountered other rocks, made small cataracts and falls. Turning a bend she found herself on a small shelf in the valley, out of which her companionable water had made quite a sizeable torrent, which swung off to the left passing an old-fashioned mill with a sullen empty wheel-pit, and a mill-race with a sluice drawing off water from the brook. Robyn was surprised to think that her spring had become an economic force, until at least the removal of the wheel, and had been so by the look of the mill from Jacobean times or earlier. As she stepped across the little wooden mill-bridge, she looked down and paused, startled. The brook was at least six feet deep and flowing powerfully, a tawny strong water.

Here the touch of summer was so hot she saw it spelt in block letters. The fact that the sluice was closed and the race dry annoyed her. The dusty odours of summer told her that the journey had been too long. She decided that she must beg some refreshment from the mill-owners, a cup of tea or some milk, which she would offer to pay for, before starting back. Robyn crossed the bridge, and just as her foot touched the further bank, a woman came out of the mill.

Robyn hesitated, embarrassed.

'Please forgive me . . . I don't mean to trespass but I've walked a long way today and I'm very hot and tired. I wondered if . . .'

The woman stood very still, looking across the garden at Robyn. She looked calm, untroubled by the heat. She wore a long brown skirt and a white smock embroidered with green leaf-patterns. Robyn fidgeted under the woman's steady gaze. The woman was tall, strongly-built in the shoulders but still slender; she was about Robyn's height, five foot seven or so, but moving as slowly, in the poised fashion that she did, seemed much taller than Robyn felt. And she was dark like a gypsy, with a low slightly simian brow broad between her eyes, which were very large and bright as she continued to stare steadily at the intruder.

The afternoon grew hotter and Robyn thought of harpies. Her heart was a small red door opening on several futures. Her thoughts jibbed, it was like trying to find something in the dark, in her head. She was frightened of this tall monkeyish woman, and couldn't decide whether she were attractive or the reverse. Robyn remembered school-friends dismembering water-lilies.

The dark woman said: 'No, please come in. At first I thought you were someone I knew, instead of someone I'm about to know! But come in please. Would you like some tea? Or some wine? I'm very glad to see you.'

The speaker had moved towards Robyn as she spoke, and now seemed about to take her arm. Instead she motioned the red-haired girl towards the mill, and led the way, pushing open a stout oak door. And Robyn moved forward, suddenly confident, feeling she knew the cool darkness of the threshold through long habit and usage. As she stepped over this threshold she gasped, seeing that the whole interior of the mill was made of books. The walls were lined with them, up to the ceiling.

'Oh,' she cried, 'my father would love to visit this place!'

The dark woman smiled to herself as she watched Robyn explore the mill. The door behind her slowly swung ajar and she took a big door key from its hook on the left hand side of the fireplace, turning it in the lock with no sound.

It was the books that chiefly amazed Robyn as she looked round. There was a broad window set in the curving wall of them, reflecting the clear hot sky. The cylinder of the mill was roofed in dark wooden beams, and here was a rough workman's ladder, old and strong, rising to an upper storey. Robyn glanced up at the stark bedroom then turned to peer through a green-curtained alcove that led into what at first seemed an ordinary kitchen. But as Robyn looked she saw through the doorway a cabinet fitted with a sink and small electric furnace, some graving tools lying on the slate working-surface, and a small electric motor fitted with a wheel clamped to the side of the bench, so that the kitchen was a kitchen-cum-workshop — she thought a lapidary's or an enameller's workshop. Robyn looked away quickly, when she saw the dark woman smiling at her. That smile robbed her of her confidence and her private magic, and made her feel like a kid.

She tried to recall the taste of water, and couldn't. With a mental shrug of her shoulders, she decided to live in this present.

On the big table under the window there were more books covering some sheets of manuscript, and an electric typewriter. Robyn couldn't decipher the subject of the big thorny writing from the quick glance that manners allowed. Robyn touched the unresponsive keys of the machine. 'You're a scholar, I see . . .' and she gestured awkwardly around the mill that was also a library and a workshop. The woman looked serious for a moment, then smiled again. Robyn decided that it was her smile that made her uneasy; it was nervous, defensive, a bit sly; could be catty, was not at any rate an expression of joy. Her face serious, in repose, was on the other hand, full of joy. 'A reader at any rate,' she answered. 'I'm Dr Hare. Brid Hare.' Robyn bobbed her head. 'I'm Robyn Treviles.'

6

Alone in Treviles Towers, the great mansion that has grown into the garden, that obstructs Fentonluna Lane, Gregory Horrorhouse weeps hot tears which are copper coins of money, stamped with the wombface of Satan. His banker enters the tear-littered room with shovel and coal-scuttle and without speaking collects debts. The banker's frock-coat glistens with dry salt. Silently he leaves the vouchers under the bronze portrait of Mamie's skull.

Gregory's two oxen are called Star and Dandy. Mamie's ghost swims in the river Reel, fully clothed. Mamie's ghost walks under three arches of yew, which is poisonous. Her passing shakes poisoned needles into the reservoir.

Gregory has been a valet to younger men. He has ducked an oil lamp thrown at him by the contessa. He has been fighting with quarter-staves. After farcical interrogations and prison meals, he was pardoned and released. An hour before execution the governor brought him his reprieve. The governor wore his face; he wore the governor's face. The governor withdrew, leaving the cell door wide open, and sat down in the armchair to watch the prisoner release himself, walk through the steel portals, and sit down with the governor in his armchair. An evening's television is no entertainment for a man in his position, it is more dangerous than paperback fiction. Shall he soon not see the currents of radio with his skin, and never be able to turn the news off? Shall all channels not come in upon him in one great blort, like a custard and bilberry pie crushing his head, or like the detailed de-programming of bodily decay?

He had the Saxon key to the doors. After the Sweating Sickness and the Great Fire which devastated the land and the people, Gregory wrote a note to Robyn, then sighed, and tore the paper up. She was delayed; she said she would be late and he was not to wait up for her, she had often slept in the open; he was not jealous; the television had hypnotised him; and perhaps he had hypnotised the television to show his own images to him on its screen. It was time for bed now, he switched off the fire; he bent down behind the television to take its mains plug from the socket. The mains plug lay on the carpet; it had never been plugged in.

7

'Books? You admire my books! They are the visible strata of my life,' said Brid. 'I wanted to be a sculptor. When I was little, I loved the touch of things, I used to model small birds in the river-mud using a quill to scribe their plumage, I would fill the edges of the little tidal inlet where the mud had grown firm enough with a veritable Noah's Anabasis of animals come down out of the mud to drink at the river. I would work along the banks until dusk and come home looking like a little mud-animal myself. Many times my mother scolded me for a tom-boy (I have no brothers or sisters) but one evening in the summer holidays she lost her patience and gave me a good hiding and put me to bed. But I would not stay in bed, I came down to where she was sitting by herself in the moonlight on the window seat and like a dog persuading its master to go for a walk I tugged her gently towards the door, and we went out to the river whose tide had not yet gathered up my animals and she saw the silver-and-black menagerie of them under the moon and she hugged me and never scolded again.

'But because I was good at modelling I was also good at drawing and because I was good at these techniques I was good at observing, and this made me good at science and I won scholarships and clearly the best thing to be was a doctor. My mother had died and I inherited the mill where we came each summer on our holidays. And here on the lowest shelves are the first books I brought home to study with and I forgot my mother and my modelling and there in pride of place is my *Gray's Anatomy* and those books of surgery mark the year I qualified because I wanted to be a surgeon at first and I read for the R.C.S. exams but then I started seeing things.'

'I'm Robyn Treviles,' the auburn-haired freckled girl had said and those feelings of her breakdown suddenly overwhelmed Brid so that she knew neither time nor space. She remembered how the whole interior of the dark mill had swirled and the books had melted and poured from the shelves and she thought she stood inside a tornado or water spout from which the only way out was down into the little brightly-coloured space full of green armchairs in each of which sat a person wearing a red cap that was also twirling, very fast, a convocation of red-capped piskies each with their left leg drawn up under thighs like the Lincoln Imp or the Imp you so often see guarding the front doors of Cornish homes. Brid sank down into this place and into the armchair and faced the red-haired person. Time had passed: there were shadows in the mill and a smell of water, not a damp odour, but a scent of evening rain, fresh and sweet. The cinnamon biscuits were out of the tin with its Trooping the Colour scene on the lid, and the empty tea cup and crumbs on a plate at her elbow said she had eaten and drunk with the red-haired girl, but she had no recollection of doing so. She blinked, shook her head from side to side groggily and said 'Yes, I've met your father. I saw him not long ago.' Then she tried to pick up the threads of the conversation that had begun with Robyn's evident delight in Brid's books and fallen into the whirling abyss of the name 'Treviles', but she found she was telling the story of her life instead: 'Books? You *admire* my books! They are the visible strata of a mis-spent life . . .'

8

Endenberg's dog bit me hard on the hand, without drawing blood. It was my right hand, the male hand. You should keep that dog under control, I said. That dog is under control, he said, smiling like God. I noticed that the grandfather clock in his hall wore antlers. There was a set of antlers hung on the wall behind the grandfather clock. We went into his study. The gas-fire was burning brightly, and he spread the documents over the velvet table-covering.

I want you to have the best part of my estate, he said briskly, getting straight down to business. There is here roughly fifty thousand pounds' worth of securities, which bring in one hundred pounds a week. For the past fifteen years I have lived on a fifth of this sum, and the rest has been passed over to my portfolio of securities, which by now must be worth considerably more than the original capital. Wouldn't you agree? he said, appealing to me.

You! I exclaimed. You! Of all people! You, buying and selling on the stock market!

Yes, he replied, it is a terrible fault for which I honestly reproach myself. And I shall reproach myself after death if you do not make better use of it than most other men would, Gregory. My purpose was to live in this house and write my book: the money I leave you, Gregory, will give you the means to carry out its instructions. If you fail me after reading my book, the knowledge in it will destroy you, there is no other way it can end.

What is the title of this book?

It is called: 'The Attainment of Deep Trance Hypnotic Conditions in Hysteric and Psychotic Subjects, with an Appendix on the Use of Jung's Technique of Active Imagination Under Trance Conditions'.

Did you write it in this house?

I looked inwards!

And can I have the antlers off your wall too? I asked sarcastically.

No, he said quietly, your antlers will be invisible, and made of gold.

What do you mean? Will I be a rich cuckold?

I hope you will learn what women and money can teach you, he answered passionately.

He beckoned and I followed him into a little dark scullery that smelt of mice.

Would you like a cup of tea? he asked

No, I said, I must be getting back, Mamie will be wondering what's happened to me.

Look at this, he said, and turned on the cold tap in the big yellow porcelain sink. Water ran jetting from the mains in a cold clear spout. As I watched, he jerked his wrist and turned the tap off hard. Then he swung the faucet open again. A spout of molten gold hissed and spattered softly into the basin. He turned the tap off and looked at me, smiling. His eyes were the colour of the gold.

I picked at a spangle of soft gold that had splashed up on to the draining board. I was speechless.

Take it home and have it analysed, he said jauntily.

He turned the tap on again. I held my breath. This time it was black water.

When this water is hot, he said, it is crystal clear, and I bathe in it. As the bath cools, the water grows black, like peat-marsh water, black and refreshing.

His leathery face that watched me with its golden eyes looked as though it had been preserved in a marsh.

When we have completed the signing of our papers, he said, I shall bathe in black water and this will bring my death to me naturally. I am three hundred years old. When you enter or leave my house, you must suffer my dog to give you his love-bite.

Treviles's right hand went out into the bed searching for Mamie. He found her face under his pillow and she bit his hand hard, but without drawing blood.

9

'Brid's story is so very unlike my own.' Robyn was beginning to understand this dissimilarity as she explored the older woman's lack of confidence, as she explored the older woman's unconfident body, building it up into itself, giving it by long slow caresses for the first time its own strong hips, restoring to it its own shoulders and long arms, its strong teats, causing the nipples to glow and prickle to themselves, offering the thighs their own pleasure, healing with pleasure the frightened wet wound between.

To Brid the images and sensations streamed past as though she were watching from a train, as though she were the train itself passing through the country that was herself that was all sensations, the turf, the trees, the grains of soil, the birds, the worms, the music of the iron tracks, the red dust of the iron shoes of the brakes that were slowly lifting their restraint from the wheels, the diesel with its pounding hum in the grilled chamber, the great coriolis winds that twisted over the flesh of her planet as it fell through space strung and vibrant with energy of the sun and the moon and all the stars. As Robyn caressed her she saw the inchoate tidal mud shiny and blubbery as a pudding, silky to touch and like bread and sawdust to smell, under the sunshine of her child's estuary, the ranks of animals and small people she built in its firmer reaches, up to her knees in it, in her ragged tom-boy shorts and aertex shirt; and this mud that was smooth, so smooth suddenly wrinkled into convulsions with a feeling of horror and became rank upon rank of books which were also pieces of corpse in the dissecting room. The pieces of corpse began to seep and bleed, dark blood and straw-coloured lymph dripped from the shelves and as she moaned Robyn's modelling of her body into itself implacably continued. The books which were eyes and fabrics of lung and legs started to revolve slowly as Robyn's hands travelled spirally around her body until they picked up speed: and Brid found herself once more inside the whirlwind, so steely by its speed that she could see herself naked reflected in its sides as she remembered a mirror that her mother kept, a shaving mirror belonging to her dead father would pull her face out into strange shapes before it settled into magnification. With a heavy rustling two magpies flew out of the mirror-walls and re-entered them on the opposite side. Her feet rested on earth and stones and the shininess of the walls now had a note which was both their shine and her pleasure, a high hum like a top she once had whose plunger you pushed down till the top rode of itself giving off a fine organ hum; these walls were like this toy of her childhood and as she remembered this many rainbow colours began to appear in the walls at first in broad bands and swirls like a coiling rainbow around her and then moving so fast that they became a warm gold colour. At the appearance of this gold they began to contract, but not alarmingly: rather as though she herself were expanding to fill her own skin, and at the same time she felt a pleasure in this skin that was so great it was also a pain, like something she had never felt before but always knew was there. The golden garment fitted her absolutely, and as it touched and entered her flesh she shrieked and bucked on the little bed in the mill's loft, her belly thrusting out, her head and her heels pushing her body away from the sheets, her eyes screwed up tight, like a person in convulsions. With a great breath she relaxed and felt cool sweat break out over all her skin, trickling from under her hairline and slowly tickling the sides of her throat. She felt also a pressure and presence, very hard and comforting, between her legs and deep within her. She opened her eyes and saw the friendly face of the red-haired girl looking at her quizzically. She reached out her right arm and drew this loved face down and kissed it softly at first, then passionately, feeling the girl's finger drawn gently out of her and the smooth body twining wholly about her own.

10

Gregory Treviles is chatting in the senior common room with Harrison, the entomologist, who wears a dark purple patch over his right eye. 'Will they get this ioniser for the church?' he asks. 'I'm not on the committee,' says Harrison, 'but I expect so. I've a good deal of evidence from my own work that insects in particular will travel and gather according to the ionic balance of the terrain. I have read that this may be an explanation for the marching of ants and the swarming of locusts. If so, the Middle East food situation will be improved, since, theoretically at any rate, you could direct the billion locusts with a negative ion beam like parting the waves of the red sea.' 'The Khamsin?' 'That is the name for the hot wind that comes off the desert. The burning sand strips off the electrons from air molecules and you get a monstrous wind, like the sirocco, that drives people mad because it is mostly positively ionised nitrogen. Jerusalem University devised small negative ion generators working off the car battery that counteracted this, filling the cabs of the lorries and the insides of the cars with this bracing, tingling electrical effect. Immediately the traffic got quieter and the road accidents went down.' 'I've never seen a generator.' 'I've seen one variety, that produces a corona discharge off a point with a battery and transformer. You've got this socket, and inside a steel needle. Put the back of your hand close to the socket, you can feel the "ionic wind". In the dark the corona is an exquisite violet glow at the tip of the needle.' 'Is that what they'll use in the church?' 'No, I expect they'll use an ionising radioactive source with a fan to circulate the air.' 'A friend told me that he has installed one in the common-room of the mental hospital he runs and there are good results, less twilight depression, fewer fights.' 'Use one in your study and you can work hours without noticing the time pass. There's a post-coital feeling in your skin all the time!' 'Worth money. How much was yours?' 'About forty pounds. You know that a candle will produce the same effect, that's why you have them on romantic restaurant tables, they help produce an erotic trance. I suppose churches burn candles for the same reason — there is a calmness and attention from the burning of a candle. Water-spray does it too — which is why the old Chinese contemplated by waterfalls.' Gregory nodded as Professor Carstairs passed by. 'I hear they've found naturally-occurring LSD in the holy well at Ruan Minor.' 'Why not.' 'Your work on insects?' 'I noticed that certain caterpillars I was studying ate more actively when the sky was cloudless. I thought this was because of the sunshine at first, but they continued to eat as actively when I shaded them. I found that the condition was that the sky should be cloudless. This made me look into the matter of ionic balance and electrostatic environment and I found some work published by our own An Cuntellow press. It seems that the earth is normally electrically charged, but negatively, and her creatures thrive. Clouds in the air are also negatively charged, so that when one passes over the ground becomes positively charged, and this inhibits the ground's creatures, who feel dull and heavy and lose appetite until it has passed over. You know what it's like with a thunderstorm impending, the seven-mile high black anvil-cloud floating over your head; the lovely freedom of the downpour and the exquisite lively air afterwards!' 'I have sometimes felt in depression in Cornwall,' replied Gregory, 'that as the black mood crept in it had the shape of a ragged cloud, and sometimes I have felt the mood slide away, and I have opened my eyes, and have seen a cloud precisely of that shape sliding off the sun. But I thought that these were "signs of reference".' 'What are signs of reference?' 'Psychiatrists' jargon for apparent coincidences experienced in manic or paranoiac states. The same as "aleatory" in art, or "serendipity" in literature.' 'What do you think?' That everything has a meaning, but if we see it all at once it's inclined to drive us mad.' 'Do psychiatrists go mad?' 'Rather more often than other folk it seems. But we try to enjoy it when it happens. There's a high rate of suicide among us, but I don't personally think that's a good advertisement for one's own psychology. As a scientist, then, Harry, you think this skin-seeing is rational.' 'Certainly! the worm sees with its skin, and many insects do also. My own work shows that this "seeing" has to do with ionic balance, and is more intense when the air is charged with negative ions.' 'And they're putting that into the University Church! What effect will it have!' 'It's supposed to keep people awake during the service since the ventilation is so bad in there. I suppose it'll freshen up their skins. I daresay they'll enjoy Christianity more in a post-coital atmosphere.' 'I've always wondered whether the witch-nipple and the familiar that sucked at it wasn't a magnified reality, as so many hallucinations turn out to be. I wondered whether the aconite in witch-ointments, or else the lashing of the skins in their rites, the flagellation, might not sensitise the seeing of the skin so exquisitely that initiates could see the lice on them suckling them; moreover, treat them as threshold guardians to the archaic world, converse with them through their skins.' 'As an entomologist, what couldn't I do with such a skin!' 'There's a school of thought that believes the Loch Ness monster sightings and their irregularities can be explained by a kind of shifting magnification caused by the power of the water in the loch, perhaps acting on our dowsing-feelings (which I believe to be the basis of ancient water-worship, and well-worship). They say that when the currents form in a certain pattern you can see a single bacterium in your teeth, and this, projected on the outside, is the water-horse, or the Loch Ness monster. It has been maintained that this is the origin of Dragons, the strange "Worm in the Teeth" of the Egyptian Book of the Dead, the Worm that wishes to hold the Bolt of the Door in Babylonian scripture, the serpent-horses of our white English hills. You see, Harrison, if in those ancient times instead of using clumsy microscopes people could see and understand the minute organisms that attacked them, and those that were benign, and mounted a system of litanies and ritual actions that discouraged the one and encouraged the other, that would be practical religion, would it not, and an evolutionary force — preserving our organisations and their development against the ravages of disease and co-operating with the small powers whose interests were parallel with our own. Why, Badminton, the embryologist, in his book on modern art, hints that the same faculty may still be lodged in the artist, and that the basis of many so-called modern abstract works may be a vision of the artist's own cellular structure. I myself have had an obsessional patient, a young painter, whose canvasses were full of shapes I recognised from the histology course I took for my Prelims. I took a histology book out from the library and showed him the photomicrographs — he was fascinated, his drawings gained definition. At length he showed me a canvas that I saw was the pattern of the "setting" muscles of the leg, with the *peroneus longus, vastus* and the rest. One notation at the side of the picture puzzled me; its calligraphy reminded me of nerve cells degenerated by polio. I noticed my patient walking with a limp. Over the subsequent weeks these muscles of his leg began to wither.' 'Auto-suggestion . . .' 'Oh what's that, Harrison?' 'Did you cure him?' 'I sent him to the hospital. They did many painful electrical tests. So painful he refused to go again. A friend suggested acupuncture to him, and I suggested Vitamin E. He is quite well now.' 'His psychological trouble?' 'That left him as the leg began to wither, and has not returned with its recovery. Acupuncture is difficult for a Western doctor to accept, all our training goes against it, we are brought up to study visible structures, visible in the cadaver, discoverable in the dissecting room. Acupuncture speaks of a webwork and ganglia of positive and negative forces over the skin, a balance of bright yang and dark yin, like your positive and negative ions. I have seen a film of a chest operation, the chest lying open like a butcher's shop and the unanaesthetised patient with only a few long needles stuck into his musculature laughing and eating an orange, chatting with the usual anaesthetist who has no work to do, but who nevertheless keeps his rubber mask poised in case of catastrophes. But there were none. Operating in this way is safer, there is no anaesthetic shock. Food can be taken for strength immediately before and after the procedure.' 'Science and art meet.' 'Science, art, religion meet. But often I think the beauty and depth of the visions, the responsibility they give us, will drive us all mad before we understand, stand under, them, Alice under the mushroom cloud.' 'You respect your patients then?' 'None more, Harrison, none more.'

II

'It was the *possibilities* that made me feel so mad, Robyn,' said Brid with the little defensive smile that she wore when she was talking about her breakdown. Transplants. Cosmetic surgery. Cosmic surgery. Bravura surgical feats done by the dream doctor in the locked attic bedroom. Avenues of moon stood on the river. Avenues of dawn-mist stood on the river. The head of Treviles on the slim body of Robyn, gazing down at her slight pale breasts. Brid's scalp on Treviles's chest, her long hair cascades through the front of romantic Treviles's ruffled shirt. The horns of Himself fastened to the scalp of Brid; she is the horned bride and her white head-dress looms monstrously like a sheer mountain or a glacier walking. The föetus of Robyn's baby transplanted to Gregory's thigh; the baby is born with tiny horns like rosebuds: 'Give me milk, Mummy,' he cries in Russian as he emerges. Treviles's penis transplanted to Brid's *fossa navicularis*, long enough for her to get up her own true self. Brid's tit grafted to Gregory's scrotum, to milk the horned babe. Clifford Treviles's dead eyesockets and middle fingerbones fashioned into a pair of heavy scholastic spectacles for Gregory to wear when he appears on television. Robyn's head transplanted to Treviles's tummy: they converse in the bath. Robyn enjoys the use of the lower part of Treviles's lungs, and they learn sympneumata, or the forced draught through one mouth and out of the other, so that they breathe like the birds 'whose grace is combustion'. The high temperature of their metabolism renders them capable of extraordinary mental gymnastics in their conversation, verbal tower piled on toppling verbal tower, and the bath water soon boils dry, they are talking so swiftly it is like bird song in the clouds of mist. Treviles's body studded with the sensoria of the two women: this happy man enjoys the inputs of six eyes, six ears, six nostrils, three mouths with lips, six tits, one penis and two cunts each crying out for it, and cannot find too much to do. Treviles has been shorn of all his sensoria and has been made into an egg of smooth white skin, in which pressure gathers, and which in due course will burst. The two women are given Treviles's four limbs and walk like insects on six legs each. Robyn's hand is fastened to the cervix of Brid's womb and Treviles's glans has been replaced with Brid's hand so that the two women shake hands in friendly intercourse and refuse to let go.

Robyn turned from her contemplation of the avenues of sunshine standing on the river Reel to hear Brid say: 'Dr Ronda told me that my chief fear was of not being a woman. Surgery made me mad because I wanted to give myself a man's body. I could not stop the metamorphoses. He taught me to hate the magic, to settle for a one reality, the reality accepted among folk like me. Existence was bearable that way. Otherwise it was as though somebody constantly swung the handle and changed the plots. Dr Ronda encouraged me to study as an analyst, since I knew what breakdown was like. I was to heal by putting people together, not by taking them apart. They say I'm a good ambulance-woman as an analyst, good for emergency treatment. But now you, a woman, have made love to me as if you were a man. What have you done to me Robyn?' and she began weeping into her pillow. 'Didn't you like it, Brid?' 'It was lovely . . .' 'I love you Brid.' 'I love you too Robyn.' And Robyn felt proud of her power over the older woman, and then she looked to one side of her gigantic pride, and saw that she was justly proud of the natural force Brid had elicited from her, and she dropped on her knees by the old bed where Brid was weeping and said 'Thank you, Brid,' knowing that she had completed herself and would not have to use anything but the most natural magic ever again. Though perhaps all the magic she had ever done was only natural.

12

Gregory drove to Penycumgwik that afternoon for the poetry seminar at the old Art Institute in Tanglewood Lane. He could not disengage himself from his thoughts, which were of plunging through the excited skin — excited by water, waterfalls, orgasms, anger, flagellation, custard pies — into the molecules of the body, and the strange landscapes full of lochs and monsters, and the strange powers and insights there residing. At first his thoughts were exalted as he imagined himself so sinking into the molecules like a god travelling the galaxy, full of powers over his own universe; then they took an unpleasant turn as he thought of the death of the galaxy, and the screaming hell of the disintegration of all the lovely architecture of the cell in the grave. The road and the grand Cornish landscape unfolding itself outside his car was scarcely visible to him as he thought of his brother, Marjorie's late-born child, whom he had hardly known, of his dreadful bruised mask in the coffin surrounded by a paper undertaker's frill since no more than just the front of the head could be shown, ready for the fire. Was it right to burn the dead? he wondered. If the consciousness lingered within the body and you attacked its mansions with a blort of fire like the flash of an atomic bomb, how could that consciousness learn from the changes and adjust to its new state. Or was that consciousness independent of time, as was the dreamer, or the lover who having entered his mistress would undergo manifold adventures in a few minutes or hours, it was all the same. He remembered Endenberg's lecture and his contention that the 'flu virus and other viruses, being nucleoproteins that (theoretically) could be crystallised as the tobacco mosaic virus can be crystallised, were the sparkling scale and dandruff of the bodily misfortunes of oppressed peoples — was it folk-wisdom that called it 'Mao 'flu' — perhaps all unintegrated people faced with the panic of death disintegrated into such viral crystals like a shattered windscreen, and the code of their bad thoughts blew around the world in diseases and accidents. Clifford and Marjorie lived dead in the soil. Mamie and Jon were dead ashes. Were the graveyard ghosts composites that could not find their original pattern, and this was why they gibbered? Ten billion billion bacteria nurtured on the cells of one body made up one drifting ghost. Now he saw (as he drove automatically) one great ghost with a head of a single many-faceted crystal reaching out its tendrils and fingers of mist over a sleeping town. He thought: it is the crystal virus of influenza that gives those formal abstract thoughts during 'flu, bodiless, compulsive, without depth, my brain magnifies the soulless crystal that multiplies in its depths, and these are my thoughts and actions in depression. The crystals, and the bacteria, and the mean thoughts, and the fragments of nobility rise up to us out of the molecular depths, because we are made of dead people's molecules. The obsessions of the dead show their faces, they ask us for assistance, and as we burn in our sick fevers they take our bodily substance for their fees. Their cries to us out of our depths are cries of love and pleading and hope, and if we allow them to love us more than we love them, our sickness, our disease, then they will consume us, we shall die then, and become ten billion of them immediately, and go on our travels through the ground, into the wheat, into the bread, into the bodies of the children, to set up our clamour. The fever becomes a river, into which we dissolve, and the river rises again out of the ocean in clouds of rain, and descends. The fever becomes a river of wax. It is the nature of wax to make masks. The river of wax becomes a river of masks. The nature of the river of creation is to make masks that melt and reform to utter a cry that is extinguished as the mask melts again. The name of the wax of this river is known to the doctor as 'vernix caseosa'. This term translated into English means 'cheesy varnish'. It is a substance known to doctors that covers the skin of the foetus. As doctors also know it is a substance that covers the skin of the corpse, exuded as a preliminary to the resorption back into the womb of the soil. Bones covered with cheesy varnish. The freshly dead person is struggling to remake himself out of the ten billion billion bacteria that infect us and that immediately he ceases breathing, begin eating. How then can he remake himself out of cheesy varnish, out of the mask upon mask? The masks are like the ten thousand expressions of a person changing from old age to infancy, these expressions that lie heavy upon the face of a fresh corpse, and which flit away like invisible insect swarms, piece by piece, through the long hours of the wake.

As his mind, or was it his body, spoke to him on this theme like a radio set tuned to several stations at once, his hands and his eyes steered his car to a stop under the shady trees of the raised pavement opposite the old Art Institute. A freshly-painted notice fastened to the front of the building read: 'AN CUNTELLOW: THE UNIVERSITY OF CORNWALL. DEPARTMENT OF ENGLISH AND COMPARATIVE LITERATURE. PRINCIPAL AND RESIDENT POET: PETER REDGROVE. MATRON IN CHARGE OF STUDENT WELFARE: PENELOPE SHUTTLE.'

13

'I did strange things, Robyn,' said Brid, still with that defensive little smile on her face, 'things that I've never told anybody, except Dr Ronda. He said that when the right person came along I should be able to tell that person easily and freely, but I thought he would be a man, not a woman like you. I used to come here to the mill whenever I could and dress myself in clean clothes, in dresses sometimes, long white dresses, sometimes in shirt and trousers, and I'd go down to the estuary of mud where I had made the animals, where the mud is always different, sometimes in sunshine or twilight, sometimes, and this was best, at the full moon, and I'd walk in my clean easy clothes past the sloppy mud that is coloured like chocolate stretching from bank to bank, sheets of it broken only by hand-holds of river-grass in tufts, and this might be it; my body alive with excitement and shame I'd maybe walk on if this wasn't the place, to where it was less sloppy but still shiny, it might be here; or where it became like a blancmange that if you slapped one bank the wave would travel over the taut surface and blowholes of creatures would open in it, not here; not this, perhaps that; or where it has become arranged in semi-solid billows with a slender stream running between, and it could be here; or where the banks round into an arena among grass and trees filled with brown and purple matter that quivers and over which the salty mists build, and it would be here! Here! and I'd run out on to it and sink and throw myself sprawling into the chilly plasm or the warm plasm and I would roll and carry it over all of myself, like shawls, and on the more of it I would roll more and my head would go under into blank blackness and I would rear my head up, and the blowhole would appear in my head of mud, happy monster and I would lie there silky and seal-black. Then I'd drag myself out. Sometimes there would be a little spring that had appeared where I could wash the worst off and go slapping back in my dirty wet rags, sometimes I could clean myself in the little river when it had bent in its earth near the bank, often I walked back as I was, pretending to lope like a werewolf on all fours and I'd open the mill-race (the mill's machinery is long gone) and wash myself clean and new in the fall and force of that. Many times I'd strip my clothes off in the high-falling all-in water and look down at myself as the blackness faded from my body, hoping some change had come about . . . Dr Ronda said I should go on doing these things as long as I wanted to. I thought I was a sort of werewolf. I thought that the mud was my mother and I hoped it would remake me (indeed I was remade and refreshed by these wallowings) as I had remade it into animals and men when I was a child and a sculptor, and I thought that my name 'Hare' guided me, because it is only (I learned from my books) in the hare and the rabbit that the animal's womb can re-absorb a foetus in hard times, and re-use the material; and I read about the great stags, who carry mystery about their branched head, who churn up wallows with their fore-feet in mud and peat where they roll themselves . . .' Brid turned over in the bed to her left. She could see stars out of this window in the night-time. Now she could see the sunlit tops of trees as the afternoon drew on.

'I love the deer! When we lived near Richmond Park, they were as frightening and desirable to me as the oak trees. Notices were nailed to trees and fastened to railings in June because that was when they calved and we kept well away. I seem to remember feeding deer at other times in my life, but that may be a dream. The thrill when a stag turned its great Red-Indian head with the antlers on it like the map of a river, all the points turning easily, that moment held as great a thrill as if a tree had come alive, since the grove's secrets were now at walk within it. In this memory it's always autumn, the colour of the ground is red with leaves', she turned in the bed and reached out stroking Robyn's hair, speaking directly to her, but not yet looking her in the eyes, 'the haunches of the deer are russet, and the apples that we ate at home russet . . .'

'Robyn,' she said, after a pause, 'Dr Ronda said I should do it whenever I wanted.' 'Do you want to do it now?' 'Yes . . .' 'Come on then, dear Brid.'

14

The twelve listeners frowned, as he read his poem. He spoke clearly. He revived himself by the reading. His depression vanished. There was nothing to be afraid of. The bearded chairman of the group watched him benignly.

MEMORIAL

(Jonathan Treviles: 28 December 1937 –
24 December 1957)

Two photographs stand on the dresser
Joined up the spine. Put away
They fold until they kiss each other,

But put out, they look across the room.
My brother and myself. He is flushed and pouting
With heart, and standing square,
I, already white-browed and balding,
Float there, it seems, and look away.
You could look at us and say I was the one of air,
And he the brother of earth
Who, in Christmas-time, fell to his death.

Fancy, yes; but if you'd seen him in his life
There'd be his bright blond hair, and that flush,
And the mouth always slightly open, and the strength
Of body: those muscles! swelled up with the hard
        hand-springs at night
Certainly, but strong. I, on the other hand
Was remote, cross, and disengaged, a proper
Bastard to my brother, who enjoyed things,
Until he was able to defend himself. It's June;
Everything's come out in flush and white,
In ruff and sun, and tall green shoots
Hard with their sap. He's ashes
Like this cigarette I smoke into grey dryness.
I notice outside my window a tree of blossom,
Cherries, I think, one branch bending heavy
Into the grey road to its no advantage.
The hard stone scrapes the petals off,
And the dust enters the flower into its peak.
It is so heavy with flowers it bruises itself:
It has tripped, you might say, and fallen,
Cannot get up, so heavy with dust.
The air plays with it, and plays small-chess with
        the dust.

The usual silence followed. Two of the listeners were scribbling angrily in their notebooks. The Resident Poet — chairman of the group — said:

'Thanks very much, Gregory . . .'

Gregory opened his mouth to speak but the poet held up a hairy hand.

'. . . Now please don't say anything about what you meant by the poem until we have finished talking. That way we shall get the distance between what you intended and what you actually said, which I hope will be interesting to you as the artist. Now the first thing I notice is the movement, which is slow and sad, and seems to me utterly genuine, though, against this, I also feel that some of the imagery strikes with an unholy vivacity, a kind of grotesquery: "flush and white,/In ruff and sun" for instance,' he quoted, consulting his duplicated copy of the poem.

'Surely, Peter,' said Henrietta, small, white, with a habit of nodding, 'surely that's part of the effect. There are the inner brothers in the room that kiss each other in the photograph: and the brothers in the outer world — the younger brother who has fallen into the dust and died, and the one who shoots up into the air of which he is a part and is "white-browed" like the undamaged blossom.'

'Gregory, is this about a real person?' asked Jan, white face, black fringe, long grubby skirt.

'Don't answer, Gregory, please, not yet,' over-ruled Peter.

'Well', said Alexander Bodkin in slow and measured tones, 'I think that this is a most Christian poem. "The brother of earth/ Who, in Christmas-time, fell to his death . . ." Who is that but Jesus, who came from heaven, fell into earth, his incarnation, at Christmas-time?' Gregory thought Al sounded particularly insincere, though he had no reason for believing that he was. Alicia, his wife, sat next to him, sharp-nosed, a sort of bird, with 'premature ejaculation' written all over her, thought Gregory, smugly.

'Al, don't be so phoney! You're not in your bloody pulpit now.' Alicia. 'Everybody knows that Jesus was there nine months before Christmas. I'm a mother. I know.' Alexander was colouring up and studying the carpet. 'Anyway, he was born in 5 or 6 B.C., I read it in a book of magic', squealed Alicia.

'Perhaps inside the Virgin Mari *was* heaven.'

'Then it was heaven on earth.'

'Perhaps heaven is on earth anyway, Joanna, since we all come from the wave-forms of the genetic code. Perhaps those wave-forms are heaven, the billows of heaven.'

Joanna tossed her blonde curls prettily, spitefully. 'How poetic!' she drawled.

'But intergalactic space is full of them!'

'How scientific!' pouted Joanna.

'Please let's get back to the poem, the words on the page, ladies and gentlemen, the words on the page.' The slogan was Peter's way of indicating a momentary dislike of a particular speaker. 'The poem is called "Memorial" so there's no need for us to assume that it isn't a memorial, and it's got an epigraph that reads "Jonathan Treviles" and his dates, which look like real dates to me. The poet treats of two brothers. He uses the first person nominative singular "I" which we must also presume he means, and since he's here we can't help noticing that he looks older than Jonathan Treviles would be now if he hadn't died. So we must assume he is indeed the elder brother.'

'Jonathan would have been two when Hitler's war started,' said someone very rapidly and quietly.

'Just so,' said the chairman. 'As I was saying, the poet sees the two brothers fixed in the photograph as they are fixed in memory. He is bound to his dead brother by something as close and essential as a "spine". Life goes on, trees blossom, and some branches of one of these trees fall and bruise their blossom, which dies before it matures. This is in itself a function of fertile abundance: "It is so *heavy with flowers* it bruises itself": a country sleep of death. The poem ends, please note this, with an accent of reproach and self-reproach. At least this is how I read "small-chess". I think the poet is saying that the air fingers the dead blossoms and plays with the dust as he the poet writes the poem, which he feels is pretty small beer beside the facts of death he is describing, a petty-chess; though the implication is that a resurrection both of flower and feeling is both possible and natural.'

'The function of art . . .' began Maria (round-faced, bolt-eyed, never still) angrily, stubbing out her cigarette.

'Yes . . . ?'

'Since the function of art is to raise the mind into a state where it can appreciate the events it is describing, how can you say that a poem is greater or less than the facts it describes ?'

And she rubbed her shorn hair violently, pleased to have posed this conundrum.

'You can fiddle while Rome burns . . .' suggested Peter.

'No poem ever stopped a war, Peter, or stopped a person killing themselves, or falling out of a window!'

Gregory flinched from the aggression crackling in the air. It was all he could do to keep his mind on what they were saying. He was wondering all the time what particular terrible disappointments or frustrations generated this electricity. He wanted to help. He did not envy Peter's job.

'How do you know the ways thought-in-action shown in a poem might not work on people. How do you know?' exclaimed Tivador, 'How can you know? What you do know from your own experience is that an image dropped into your mind at a receptive moment can act as the crystallisation centre round which whole passages of your life develop.' Gregory sat up. 'What is true for one person is true for the collective too. Here's a large-scale instance: the NASA space-scientists all read sci-fi, and at least one has gone on record admitting that science fiction made him decide to become a space-scientist.'

'I once met an advertising man who said he had a painting that gave him ideas for campaigns.' This was Mark, thickset and badger-grey, a Leeds voice. 'He kept it hanging across the room from his desk with a little curtain covering it that worked from a button. Whenever he was stuck for an idea he pressed the button and the painting appeared and he got his idea. He said it never failed. He was very successful.'

'I hope it wasn't the thalidomide advertising campaign,' snapped Maria, glad to be snapping again.

'I also heard an almost identical testimony from a theatrical producer,' went on Mark, quite unflustered, 'who said he had no time for "Transmitted Meditation", though he liked the Guru's smile, particularly as his own salary was so large that he couldn't afford to give a week's money as a sub for initiation. He said that he had too many actors to support. The way he meditated, he told me, was with the aid of a good book of modern verse. Reading the poetry made the play produce itself — the reverie was a calm, into which clear ideas walked. He claimed to be able to use an ancient Chinese dictionary also.'

'I wonder if reading poetry lowers your metabolism, blood-lactate and breathing-rate like TM', said Mr Willis, the chemist.

'I wouldn't want to use anything the American Army was keen on,' said Rose, who was studying to be a nun.

Al Bodkin cleared his throat and leaned forward, staring into Gregory's face. Gregory stared back.

'Although I am myself a Christian, as you all know, and I still maintain that this is a Christian poem, or the poem of one who yearns to be a Christian, I believe there is exceptional aggression in that word "bastard" in the middle of the poem, though one could maintain that Jesus himself was in the strict meaning of the term a "bastard" since the Blessed Virgin was not actually married to the person who gave her the child. However. Neither do I like this sudden switch to cigarette-smoking among the raging fertility of June. I think this poem is a confession of guilt.'

Alec must realise that I am gagged, that I must not speak, it is as though he is speaking to my photograph, does he have a photograph of me by his bed and plead with it and God each night on his knees to send me a good Christian conversion, Gregory asked himself savagely. He would never dare if I had my tongue.

'I'm sure that you have something there,' the nun-student, Rose, joined in the attack, she was very tall, and through half-closed eyes she appeared to have two pairs of thick dark eyebrows, her eyes were in upper and lower brackets, the one pair of thick hair, the lower made of the dark pigments of wakefulness, 'the horrible suggestiveness of the boy that had to swell up his muscles with nightly exercises to defend himself against the cross remoteness of his brother-so heavy with muscles, perhaps that he fell to his death, so heavy with defences — this world is imbued with guilt so much that the innocent blossoms and the defenceless dust are images of his brother — murder, he cannot seek peace of mind in God so he seeks it in a cigarette, nervously smoking and finding a corpse even in his butt-end as he does so! This poem is misnamed, all the poems of this author are mis-named. The title of these works should be "The Terrors of Dr Treviles!"' Her eyes glared from black sockets.

Six voices broke out at once, Henrietta, Mark, Maria, Josie, Alec and Joanna:

'I think it's phoney, like most memorials.' (Maria)

The imaginary Albert Memorial is planted in the middle of a real garden!' (Mark)

'I think he ought to have broken some taboo.' (Josie)

'You believe he should accuse God, for inventing death?' (Alec)

'The blossoming outside is like a god of death, all beautiful on the one side, all decaying on the other.' (Henrietta)

'The Goddess! Blodeuwedd! It means "Flower-Face".' (Joanna)

'If it means Flower-face she'd have to be he-she, since blossom is dioecious, bisexual,' said Peter, 'All gods are dioecious, proper ones that is.' The hour was nearly over, and it was this chairman's custom to end the meeting with one member smarting, one scapegoat a meeting, in rotation. 'Who knows how the Christian God propagates? Reverend Bodkin. Do you know, Alec?'

What I know is that Gregory loves his brother', said Alexander firmly, still watching Gregory, 'and his brother-man, and envies him, not for dying, but for his sheer earthy presence. Whoever forced him to earth we don't know, and perhaps the poet doesn't know who to blame either — I certainly don't —God, or man, or nature or family — but for all that I think the poem has heart and regret, and in writing it the author was determined to become more like the brother he envied,' still staring at Gregory, Gregory thought, with the fixity of a blind man.

'Thanks, Al,' said Peter, looking rather taken aback, 'Now, Gregory, would you like to tell us what you meant by the poem in the few minutes remaining to us?'

15

The sculptor's bin is rucked. The sculptor has taken his clay in handfuls, for it has been lying idle too long, and has become heavy, lazy and unresponsive. The sculptor grips his clay and tears it off its bulk digging with his strong fingers, he lifts the clay and he flings it back into the bin, he grips it and he lifts it out again, and he flings it at itself with a slapping detonation. Before it has time to settle back in its inertia and idleness he plucks it out again and throws it down again. The vitality of grip, and of his blows vibrates through the clay which becomes a living thing and responsive like plasm to his fingertips and the wishes in his fingertips. The clay is purple and black as it lies rucked in its bin through which a small clear stream bends, it is surrounded by turf banks and trees. Two living shapes separate themselves in the clay, they cannot stand, they are not made below the knees, they waver and fall, and roll themselves into more of themselves. The night is coming on, the air is violet and full of the smell of plants readying themselves for the night and full of the smell of mud which is that of a deep and heavy blossom like some tropical plant. It is twilight, glimmering along the path comes a brown and white collie followed by a man dressed like a gentleman farmer in tweeds whose tobacco adds to the night scents. The clay lies still in rucks. The dog riddles along the path, the man strolls past the open bin of clay occupied with his thoughts, the dog pauses and sniffs at the very edge of the bank towards two billows in the mud that lie as still as all the rest of the mud. The dog points with his nose to these two billows and cocks his head towards his master who strolls on. A whistle loops round the neck of the dog and pulls him on his master's strolling path, though his nose would prefer to remain in contemplation of the two billows or bolsters that are mud and more than mud.

Darkness gathers among the trees and in the undergrowth. Two shadows dark as the shadows lope darting behind trees and through the undergrowth. Where they touch the light barks of trees they leave darker shadows, they have left a trail of dark shadow-prints across the pathway on which the man and the dog strolled in the twilight. Two lovers, a man and a girl, pass by, head-on-shoulder, arm-round-waist, oblivious to all except each other, or, rather, oblivious to everything that does not answer them in each other and in the outer world: her hair smells of the damp evening in the woods, his hand is strong as the bark of the trees. They falter as they pass a copse of trees and turn their heads towards the shadows; two shadows stand in the copse dark and still as the trees.

The moon in its first quarter rises. A round pit in the masonry of the mill shadowy with streaks of moonlight, it is the place made for the mill-wheel and though the wheel has gone, the runnel of the mill-race worked by a sluice still remains. There is a creaking in the night and it is as though a dark curtain has been drawn aside in the wall of the pit and white light is showing through. It is the white water of the river falling through into the pit. In the moonlight two black shadows appear in the dim masonry pit, they are two black women dressed in heavy black robes that drip black shadows. They step into the white fall and, as if a dark hoop had been drawn down over each figure revealing light, two white women dressed in wet white robes appear in the fall, appear in the small force of water, which stands over them itself like a figure in robes that cleans them. They pirouette in and out of the water, the moon goes in behind a black cloud and they are barely visible, the moon springs out of her darkness and they shine with brightness.

Robyn lies back in her chair, skin tingling with the night, the earth, the water, her eyes closed. Brid leans over her friend and lifts up her new cotton skirt, and peels off her pants. Robyn murmurs but does not open her eyes. Brid strokes Robyn's thighs and lower belly until Robyn begins to moan and shiver. When Brid touches the fixed star of Robyn's clitoris, the girl cries out but her eyes are still closed. Brid kneels between Robyn's legs as Robyn sprawls back in the chair and gently rubs Robyn's hard hot clitoris and tickles her wet cunt. Robyn gasps, 'Yes!' running her hands over Brid's hair. Brid blushes scarlet and laughs aloud with pleasure as Robyn bucks in her chair, her legs shooting out and jerking. Robyn opens her eyes and smiles at Brid, the two smile equally at each other.

Lying now on the bed, they talked. They had known each other awake for thirty hours, now they would sleep together, and dream together.

'Will Gregory worry?' asked Brid.

'No, we go as we please.'

'Do you worry about Gregory?'

'More than he does about me.'

'I think he is a very clever man.'

'I don't know.'

'Isn't he?'

'Yes, I love him. I don't think he has merits in the ordinary sense.'

'But he's very intelligent.'

'How can you tell? His intelligence is never free from terror, or his love.'

'He has helped people.'

'They would not let him rest.'

'I don't understand. Do you mean he is unhappy? Is he difficult to love?'

'I mean that he's like a man who has jumped into the deep end and is calling out to his friends shivering on the brink, "Come in! The water's — *terrifying!" I* think it's a brink we'll all have to face some time. Something has pushed him in sooner than others, somehow. Will you come and live with us, Brid?'

'Will he like that?'

'Of course!'

16

The air of the seminar room had grown very damp and clinging, and he was glad to leave. They should leave a negative ioniser on, he grumbled to himself, and everybody would be brighter. He could not remember in detail what he had said about his poem on Jonathan, except that his death had really happened — after a party he had tried to open the flat of the girl he was with by climbing outside to get through the windows, but had slipped and fallen into the area; the pathologist had said he was not drunk when this happened — and Gregory could write nothing about it until nearly a year afterwards. He described how he could not cry; how he only felt sick when Mamie had served him boiled eggs before the funeral, since these reminded him of Jon's shattered head; how his position as one of the chief mourners at the funeral service gave him a shameful feeling of excitement and self-importance, and that this caricature feeling stood in front of deep grief, like a garishly-painted door giving on to the bank of a fast-flowing river. The opening of the door came at the end of the funeral, when the wreaths were laid. Treviles saw that one of the biggest wreaths came from Jon's comrades in the barrack-room. It was a great sword of flowers. It suddenly became apparent to his grief that Jon's ceremonial sword, cleaned and honed and polished for the parades on horse, the deathly instrument, the stiff and glittering symbol of command and law, had on his death, burst into flowers and blossom. The garish door swung aside, and the river of grief flowed. He had tried to write about this feeling in short poems but they had not worked — with the possible exception of one that spoke of the sword as mirror, and of the ten thousand things it had reflected in its life, but it was only the flowers that had the power to break through from the mirror-depths of death — and it was only one June, sitting down smoking a cigarette, he had seen Jon's corpse growing out of the fire of his smoking, at the tip of the butt, for he had been cremated; and he had looked out of the window and seen Jon's face softly and cheerfully looking in at him out of the blossom. This was the first of his terrors.

Close textual response he had given none, it was the aggression in the air, the soft damp clinging of it shot through with short bolts of helpless malice, that had distracted him, he thought that it was not only the burning sand of the desert that spoilt the air, but the burning desert of disappointed stubborn people — and was this not what the desert sands were made of, the ruins of fertile cities? Why then (this was the puzzle) should he consider himself exempt? He didn't, but he thought himself fairly free from malice because he was usually so frightened of the things his imagination told him could happen to people. He checked himself — he wasn't even free of malice, not in his relationship with Alexander, anyway.

It was time to drive home. The seminar had relaxed him, though he thought that was largely the relief of having got away from it. He felt as though he had been caught in a great thicket of cotton-wool, a soft thorn-thicket of impeding, weakly-detaining brambles. It was as the Chinese told stories of the Tangling Ghosts lying in wait for travellers, it was the deterioration of a group-mind, the last, negative stages in group therapy when the members were ready to gather themselves together and leave because they were tired of each other. He wondered about the spoors and traces of such groups that might be left in houses, or littered about the countryside from quarrelsome family picnics: he thought he had often felt these on his walks, guarding the entrance to a wood, sited at the edge of a meadow, in the shadow of a hedge. Could these tangle-ghosts be dispersed by an ionic gun? Is the air of Cornwall an ionic jungle littered with these carcasses beaded and winking with scavengers? Infested with ionic tigers pacing the ionic underbrush powered by great sinews of positive ions. Teeth made of positive ions deleterious to me? Does the positive ionic tiger pounce on me and carry off my natural negative ionic body? Am I then exhausted and depressed until I can grow a new one over my skin? Or do the two charges cancel each other out, and, unlike fleshly tigers, the tiger made of positive ions must dine on negative ions not because he is wasting with hunger, but because he is becoming too large, and drifting in breezes, pulled off balance by gusts, drifting in the wind, instead of running compact along the ground like some animal in a cartoon that has swallowed the air-line of a garage and swells and swells until it is a great zeppelin floating among the clouds marked with limb-teats and a tiny astonished Sylvester-face somewhere high up on the taut fabric. Far down below a triumphant mouse hugs its stomach with raucous joy.

Are there in the jungle swart swamps of positive ions? And refreshing negative ion waterfalls, glades, and fruiting forests?

Is there a negative ion Tarzan fighting the positive cannibals? Is there a strange ionic woman of the glades whose charged hand spreads over my depressed skin, and whose ionic fingers sink gently through my chest and massage my tired heart, as now I feel a great charge of energy coming from I know not where? I will visit the S-shaped ponds, decides Treviles as he eases himself behind the steering-wheel and elects not to fasten his seat-belt. Are there ionic marriage-beds and clergymen in this jungle of misty lianas and brilliant electrical monkeys, who truly merge two persons into one electrical body? Whole congregations into the mystical body of their church?

Certainly there are! Experience shows it! Certain places hum with a quiet song, and the green is fresher there, and there are more berries and mushrooms. This is how Harrison, the entomologist, described the S-shaped ponds at Devoran: they were the sanctuary of a certain rare sandy-haired moth that had almost died out in this country and was found only beside certain lochs in Ireland, where the ionic conditions were right, and inhabiting the weeds of the S-shaped ponds of Devoran, in Cornwall.

Treviles thought of a loch whose water was always fresh. On the floor of Loch Treviles lay the Reviled Monster. It was nevertheless the action of this Monster sluicing the used water through its gills that filled the whole waters of the loch with oxygen and kept it fresh. The Secret Monster whom all revile is anaerobic, fresh air burns it like acid, it excretes fresh air. We breathe what is poison to it, and our poison freshens it; its excretions give us health, and its health depends on our excretions.

This is why the loch with no outlet to the sea is crammed with fish, upon which we feed, upon which the Monster also feeds. We are commensal, we feed at the same table, though the Monster inhabits its dark, and we walk on the loch banks in the sunshine. Because the water is so well oxygenated, like a huge aquarium, very little weed grows in it. It is a gigantic basin of slate, shaped like half a wheel. The basin holds very clear waters, and is of immense depth. A certain green weed grows like close-cropped curls close to the stone, and this is eaten by enormous water-snails, creatures who are always fertile, who are dioecious, male-female, and whose eggs provide abundant food for the smallest fish, those at the tapering end of the food-chain.

Every autumn we take hundredweights of fish out of Loch Treviles, enough to feed our village-community and prosper the village of Treviles with its church and post-office and unspoilt green with the great oak dropping acorns in its centre, and the water-trough. The fish is exported south of the border, and we divide the profits equally among our number. Who are we? We are authors and scientists when we are not fisherfolk. We live a little apart from the world, but our researches on the brink of the Loch benefit it. We attribute our alert intelligences, our physical and emotional health, our decent fertility and equilibrated birth-rate, the absence of quarrels and factions in our small community, to our diet of fish meat and fish liver and fruit from our orchards dunged with fish manure. One of our most famous sons is Gregory Treviles. In the world, is he known? No? He is known to us.

It is prophesied that at the end of the world our Monster will rise to the surface of the Loch, writhing and thundering in the air that is like acid to her, and that she will utter the last trump with her death-cries and these will shatter the bones of the unjust.

It is also said that our Monster is simply one enormous bacterium that has mutated, and grown to this dinosaur-size, and is referred to in the Bible as 'Leviathan'. Get into the dinghy with us. Come out on to the Loch. If the sunlight is bright and strikes at the right angle you may glimpse her purple flank lying far down through the water.

Gregory walked towards the S-shaped ponds, leaving his car in the lane. The ragweed of the S-pond is the refuge for this certain rare sandy-haired moth. Drop this moth into a killing-bottle and it will scream as it touches the pearly lining of cyanide. Stopper the jar, and feel the scream running through the glass, silently, like a chill on the edge of pain, entering the bones of your hands and forearm. Abruptly, the scream will cease, but the moth will continue to fly round and round inside the jar. Harrison has recommended Treviles to search out the S-ponds and try to kill one of these moths, since Gregory was a man interested in marvels. Watching him through his eye-patch, Harrison warned that occasionally a moth ruptured the jar in its agony. He told Treviles seriously that his own killing-bottle had burst in his hand, and a splinter of glass had lodged deep in one eye. It was the end of his stereoscopic vision, and so the end of his active collecting days, since he could not wield a net in three dimensions any longer.

Are the tear-glands intact, wondered Treviles as he walked towards the ponds, having left his net and killing-bottle in the boot of the car. Ragweed was well established on the waste ground near to the pond. *Ambrosia artemisiifolia*: the food of the gods with the arrow-shaped leaves of Artemis, thought Gregory, as he walked through the three-foot high grass with the sand-coloured flowers hidden among fretted leaves.

As he approached, he heard a small multiple shrieking in the air, and the flowers left the stately plants and fluttered high up above his head. 'There are the moths.' He caught his breath.

No, he would not disturb or destroy them. He lay down among the roots of the ragweed, hugging the warm earth, and he listened. The small jets of high noise ran rhythmically across his plot of earth, and he concentrated fiercely, attempting to penetrate the sound. Time passed, how long he couldn't say, but the sun was almost ready to set and the shadows long when he began to distinguish these words, spoken very slowly:

'R-E-N-D Y-O-U-R G-A-R-M-E-N-T-S R-e-n-d y-o-u-r g-a-r-m-e-n-t-s a-n-o-t-h-e-r m-o-u-n-t-a-i-n a-p-p-r-o-a-c-h-e-s'

Then there was a long pause broken only by a noise like static or slow morse-code, and then:

'I-t i-s s-h-e A-t-t-e-n-d h-e-r'

And there was in these words an indescribably mournful strength that caused Gregory to rise from the ground and get stiffly to his feet. He saw, through the twilight, a sandy-coloured column approaching him through the ragweed. It was still a couple of hundred yards off, like a dust-storm in the desert containing a darker nucleus, but from it came a shrill note that numbed his ears. He backed away from it, turned and broke into a stumbling run but with his head turned back over his shoulders watching the cloud. He reached the car. He turned to face the column, one hand clutching the door-handle in case he was attacked by dust or locusts — in Cornwall? As the apparition passed the margin of weed, the moths fell away from the figure and there was Brid Hare in a light summer dress, a straw hat, and carrying a basket of flowers. 'Dr Hare! Brid! what are you doing out here?' but she passed by without noticing him, and moved on into the shadows of the trees in silence.

END OF PART TWO

Part Three

Robyn and Brid and Mamie to Gregory

I

Like a splash of red hair on a white pillow, the setter, Gabby, sprawled luxuriously on the hearth-rug, sleeping. Robyn and Brid sat at the table, leafing through notebooks and diaries. Gregory had eaten very little during dinner, and drunk water only. Immediately the meal was finished he left the room without a word. The two women accepted that he intended no surliness; Robyn knew from former times that he was doing his best to compose himself, to enter as deeply as he could into himself. When Brid had arrived with her suitcases, Gregory embraced her silently and helped her upstairs with her luggage. He accepted completely that she was there to stay indefinitely. But he spoke little. The voice he used was calm and low, but monotonous, like that of a deaf man. Like a deaf man too, he sometimes spoke abruptly, and too loudly.

Robyn opened a notebook of last year, exclaimed, and said: 'Look, Brid. Here's a photograph of Gregory, he is staring through a broken window. I remember, I took it when they knocked down the old Rectory. The roof had long gone, willow-herb and small trees made a copse in the living-rooms. We loved the garden inside the house. It is so strange. Do you see, Brid? It looks as if Gregory had broken the window so that we may see him more clearly.'

Brid glanced at the photograph neatly pasted in Robyn's notebook. 'Did he break the window then?' 'No, it was like that. Village boys I expect. He looks sad.' 'Sad? I don't think so.' Brid tried not to speak impatiently, after all, Robyn had known him so much longer. 'People looking out from within always look sad to me,' explained Robyn. Then she squealed and the dog Gabby got abruptly to its rust-coloured legs, she had knocked the candle over as she turned to face Brid and both women had to rescue the books and papers which lay scattered across the table. Luckily only a sheet of carbon paper shrivelled and Robyn rubbed butter on the little burn on her thumb.

In his room, Gregory also had a candle lighted to act as an ionic bonfire against prowling positive ion tigers. The doors had closed in his mind and he felt shallow, depressed. He felt that there was a build-up going on behind those doors, and that unless he opened them quick, the sea-gates would burst, flooding his land with salt water, sowing salt through his fertile fields and sterilising them beyond his lifetime. Such thin transparent thoughts as he had turned implacably towards Mamie — he could see her again as when he first knew her, red-haired in her army nurse's uniform. She showed two-dimensional, and the memory carried a stickiness and an odour to it, as though she were photographed or painted on a sheet of gelatine. The candle was burning with a red tinge, and he had an abrupt vision of Mamie squatting within the candle-flame, grinning and talking to him in a voice so tiny and fast he couldn't make out what she was saying, squatting as though she had hitched up her white skirt and pulled down her black nurse's knickers and was enthroned on the toilet, or like the Piskie, cross-legged like a tailor. What is the female for Piskie? The wick is her anus, the flame her body, always changing, ever flowing, always the same shape, always able to appear in that shape anywhere as if, for instance, I touch the candle-flame to the curtains, thus!

The curtain was only lightly scorched. Gregory returned to his chair, and put the candle down again on the desk. My mind is asking me to reverse its direction, a taboo needs breaking, I shall go under unless I do something for God I don't want to do, saying God's prayer backwards won't do, then he had a small pleasurable memory of a dream in which two people brought him forward to a white-clothed table laid with the best silver and glass for an elaborate meal. They escorted him by his elbows, one on each side. Then one of them, the woman, took some jam from a dish and rubbed it in his face, which made him feel sexy. Then he had a memory of his mother washing his face. He could feel the rough flannel and the cold water.

Gregory knew that Robyn's way of stopping the river of her mind and making it flow the other way was her rite with candles and the Lord's Prayer; he knew that, like some savage tribe making rain or mourning for the death of a queen, gentle Brid wallowed in the great abundant mud; he had found his way in the reveries after sex, or in taking an image from a dream and allowing it to take root again in his mind. Something more was needed at this moment.

He looked at the pile of pages that were his new poems. God wants something to read, he said. Mamie is sitting in the candle and wants something to read. He took the first poem and fed the corner of it into the candle-flame. It scorched and turned back from the flame. Treviles pushed it in further. With a slight detonation the page caught, red and yellow flame ran over it like the eye-beams of readers. The typed verses showed very black in the firelight, then silver as the paper's blackness soaked over them. Treviles dropped the curled flaming ash into the metal waste-paper bin and picked up the next page. God has put on his spectacles and is reading these poems. Mamie is reading these poems. God is reading these poems in the tent of the flame, which is his tabernacle. Mamie is now holding my poem and God is reading it over her shoulder. Mamie and God are only able to read my poems if they are good poems, that is if they are poems about Mamie and God. Then they do not need the pages, for they have them by heart. But every kind of poem, good or bad, will burn, says Treviles, feeding another page into God's ionic wigwam.

She makes a bonfire of her wardrobe and jewellery. Mamie rakes the ashes away from the soil in the bonfire-place in the kitchen garden and scoops a small crater. She enjoys the wet-ash smell. In the crater she contrives a small grate or hearth of her wooden clothes-hangers. Upon this she arranges her shoes, the plain sensible ones she uses for walks, the boyish ones she had worn at school, the spangled evening shoes and the fashionable roman sandals. She sighs, and places on top of these her pink bedroom slippers their rims lined with fur-fluff, and finally her long white leather boots with the six-inch heels.

Within this pile of shoes she now places all her underwear. Her plain white cotton knickers, her purple honeymoon knickers edged with Honiton lace, her blue nylon knickers, her flowery Marks' knickers, her black nurse's bloomers. Then her bras, the white, the black, the french; her flesh-coloured tights, and two vests left over from her schooldays.

On top of these flimsies, she arranged her jerseys and cardigans, her V-necked pullover in khaki cashmere, her black polo-necked jersey for riding, the cardigan with the military-style collar.

Then she unscrewed the paraffin can and poured oil into these garments. This also was a smell she enjoyed. She got up off her knees and went into the house. She came out almost immediately with an armful of skirts, long tweedy skirts, a red velvet skirt with flounces at the hem, three mini-skirts, one polka-dotted, one striped and one black, three pairs of jeans and a pair of corduroy hotpants.

She threw them on the heap, and went back into the house.

She brought out her blouses, flowered and plain, with puffed sleeves, severe pink blouses with button-down collars, classic paisley blouses, ruffled black silk blouses like theatre chocolates. There was a boy's shirt she often wore in bed, and three tee-shirts decorated with the unsmiling faces of Beethoven, Sylvester the Cat, and Elvis Presley.

She heaped these on her pyre which was a fire-wardrobe, and went back into the house.

She came out with her dresses, which she laid on the fire, like a garnish: there was the blue voile dress with the pearl buttons, the little black churchly dress, the long white party dress, the lamé dress and the brocade, the thin summer cottons with their whorls and flowers, the warm navy-blue wool suit for the office, and two nylon nighties one red, one black, each with stiff flowers on the bodice.

It took three matches to catch the fire alight, and she pulled out a pair of cotton pants which she dipped in the paraffin and used as a spill. She saw the dresses writhing, trying to get free, she saw the arms of her blouses raised in despair, the crotch of her jeans charged with fire, the bras blackening like a negro mother. The flames leapt up and the fire wove for itself a heavy hood of slaty smoke. The lancing flames were now taller than she was and she pulled off her slippers and threw them into the fire. She pulled off her dressing-gown and threw that in as well, and now she stands naked, basking in the good heat of her finery. Calling out to her 'What are you doing! Mamie!' Gregory ran out of the house. 'I'm dead, Gregory,' she cried joyously, 'I don't need clothes any more. I'm everywhere!' and stepped into the fire.

I had to burn her clothes when she was dead. I couldn't give them away or sell them. I didn't want the two-dimensional memory of these clothes. You have to burn them. I don't need these poems any more. Looked at from one angle this is a candle-flame. Looked at from another it is Mamie. The flames have her clothes, and she can wear them if she likes, she can say my poems to me if she likes.

The beeswax candle splutters and hisses.

The man watches, his head cocked, as if listening to a far-off voice.

2

'What is Maya?' asks Gregory. They are in bed, all three. They are not sleepy.

ROBYN: *Do you mean Moiré?* This morning, I was convinced that I had seen the secret of the universe in the string vest of the little boy next door, as it hung on the washing-line in the rain. The two layers of string lattice moving across each other in the breeze made moiré patterns that pulsed in waves across the garment, magnifying and pulling tight each aperture like a cat's cradle. It seemed to me that the moiré patterns of a hologram cylinder looked like this, only they are still and this is in motion. I know that if I switch on the laser set for wave-front reconstruction holography I shall see standing in the apparatus an image in full colour, in depth and height and thickness, and that if I move my head to look further round the image, if it is a picture of my dead mother, for example, I shall be able to see the glints in the patent leather of her black handbag move as I move, and I shall be able to see the seam of her stocking as it climbs up the back of her leg. If she happens to be photographed reading a paper or a poem, by craning my neck I can see also the headlines of that day's news or the lines of verse, even though she seems photographed from the front where these sights are normally invisible. I know you remember the shine of her hair as you break the gleed in the fireplace, Gregory, and how this action as the grey embers gash rose-red lights up her photograph in the place of honour on the mantelpiece. The red hair in the colour photograph is garish, and this is all the two-dimensional cardboard will carry. You will need a three-dimensional picture for the true likeness, a colour hologram you could turn, Gregory, to see the life and the lights in her hair. But then you would fear the head tilting, the lips smiling, and that she would talk to you. But why be afraid of her? Of Mamie?

The lips in the photograph are slightly parted, and as your hand passes in front of it to take a cigarette or one of your pipes, do you not fancy you feel a breath on the back of your hand?

I hold the hologram plate in my hand and I study its moiré patterns. I think of the pulsing patterns in the moiré of the little boy's string vest, and I think of how the probability patterns of the waveform atom, yin in the electron shells and yang in the tight bright nucleus, make moiré patterns; and the molecules of ordered pattern made up of these atoms make moiré patterns of moiré patterns, and these we know as emergent properties. Sodium is a silvery metal that explodes; chlorine is a burning yellow gas; the moiré of one on the other — and they flame as their patterns interpenetrate — gives the salt of wisdom, the sodium chloride of our food and tears, and its taste is of the moiré, moiré moving on moiré. That most orderly of molecules, DNA, that spindle singing with packed in its double helix all the moirés upon moirés that build my eyes, his nose, her hands, is as though I moved this hologram plate in a pattern of four dimensions, the fourth being its rate of movement in time. So, given the orderly beat of some reference beam, as the sun rises and sinks in day and night, and the seasons, and the moon moves in her day and her year, this three-dimensional molecule would give a four-dimensional image unfolding in space-time.

Look at this rose, how it unfolds from its centre. Plunge deep within this centre, plunge also back into time to the seed of the rose, at the centre of this seed you will find the moiré pattern of the rose's genetic code. This rose that you see, this scent that you smell, is the true condition and the magnified state of the molecules of the rose.

And a man? Lop-sided, diseased, neurotic, mad, vicious? Where are the perfect unfoldings of his moiré patterns, where is the promise of the womb? Where is the wholeness of his unfolding nature? Deep within, in the moiré patterns, and when we dream, this is the conscious unfolding of these patterns to us, dreams are the replay of our genetic code, that is the jargon, our possibility and our love.

What brings us here, dreaming awake in this house, venturing our souls to perfect them? Gregory has the dreams; I have the jargon; and who is to say which of these is the more useful? I say that the whole process which brings us here in the one slate bed, began with the sun beaming down complex disorder in long yearly pulses, and in its cycle of sunspots, with the moon pulsing out a shorter monthly order, the two co-inciding at the winter solstice every nineteen years, as in the pattern of Odysseus' wave-haunted wanderings.

These complex moirés registering in the very small, at the centre, on the atomic level at first in its pattern of yang for the sun and yin for the moon, then on the molecular level, combine with the pulses of the planets. Thus we have in infinitesimal compass the configuration of the solar-system, the moirés of these great bodies' interactions are reproduced on the level of the very small. All earth-matter combines to magnify, complete and extend these patterns, asymmetry revealing some further, greater symmetry, and we, man and woman, are the resultant of this process, and we are the sun and moon and the planets walking about on the earth. *That is Maya, Gregory.*

He turned in the great bed to look at the other woman. 'What is Maya, Bridget?'

BRID: *Sculpture. Maya is sculpture.* This M stands for modelling, and mud, and mother.

'I sometimes think that I could write six odes on any subject at any time,' Gregory was wild-eyed and gestured wildly pacing around my studio, he was in a mood that makes portraiture difficult. 'I shall write six odes on your new loaf of bread, if you like, or about your cheese.'

I went on carving the stone, without answering him. I wanted the cuticle of the nail and the curve of his left eyelid just so; it would carry the whole of him.

'If I wished,' he bragged, 'I could call out a legion of small black spiders to carve me a sandwich from that loaf, with that knife which they would heft by combining their minute strength, simply by reading them the correct poem. And if the spiders did not already exist in your studio, your stone dust would hatch into stone spiders on my reading this poem with its patterns of vibration like moiré patterns cutting across each other. When the stone spiders had cut me a sandwich, I would pose, and they would then carve me a portrait.' He sat back and laughed spitefully.

'You see, Brid, by composing and reading my poems, I have caused you to work for me. By the action of my poems, you have conceived a feeling for me, which must become a portrait. I have also discerned in the stone I brought you that it is a stone that wishes to become a man, and the reading of my poems, through you, is to be his liberation.'

I bent my head and thought to myself that when I had finished my work, the stone would speak better words than the poet, and the poet would fall into a silence deeper than the voices of his poems. He guessed my thoughts.

'No!' he cried, 'you haven't the power.' He spoke excitedly. 'You are infecting me with your silence, Brid, it won't work . . .'

He ceased as I held up his portrait. I had shaped the stone into the pattern of a narrow chin and a broad forehead. On the brow were two small buds. Two deep marks cut into the lump of stone woke the face, no longer a stone it watched and considered by virtue of these two deep gravings.

Gregory stood with the stone held in his hand. He raised it to his forehead and passed it across his brow two or three times. 'This is the image of my dream,' he said . . .

Brid said, *'What is Maya, Gregory?' 'Yes,' Robyn repeated, 'what is Maya?' There was a scratching at the door. Gabby pushed the bedroom door open and leapt on to the bed, settling at the foot of it.*

GREGORY*:* Macintosh on the chair, galoshes under it, umbrellas propped against it. Tiger-rug on the floor, family photographs on the piano and on the wall. A good but dull landscape above the mantelpiece. A photograph of a red-headed girl. She stares out into the camera. She hugs a red setter puppy. This is the room the family keeps vacant at eight p.m. every day, summer or winter. No one at all uses the room then.

A visitor arrives, a summer visitor. He is to inspect the books, perhaps offer a price. His host shows him round the house.

'That room? We never stay in that room at this time of day.'

'Why not?' asks the visitor.

'Another world touches it,' says the host.

'Ha Ha', says the visitor.

His host exchanges a glance with his wife, who shrugs.

'The room may bring good luck to you, if you have the courage, but the two minutes you are alone in here are likely to last a long time, too long for you perhaps.'

'I'll chance it,' says Treviles.

So they left him alone. He took the macintosh off the chair and sat down. The french windows opened and the red-headed girl of the photograph stepped in. She was very beautiful. Her hair was as red as blood.

'Sorry,' she said lightly, 'I didn't know anyone was in here, it's usually empty at this time of the day. Did you want to meet my father?'

'No,' answered Gregory, 'I'm just waiting here at the forbidden hour to see what happens.'

'Are you?' she said enviously, opening her eyes very wide. 'Can I wait with you?'

'Be my guest.'

The young girl sat cross-legged on the tiger rug. They waited in silence for an hour by Gregory's watch. Nothing happened.

'Oh dear,' sighed the girl, 'there you are, nothing happens. It's just father's way. Come and have some supper.'

They left the room and rejoined the family. Father eyed his daughter pensively for when he saw her with their visitor, it was clear to him that she had fallen in love. Gregory asked her father's permission; he agreed with only a moment's hesitation. They were married in the family chapel. The girl was already pregnant but everybody was very happy. On the way to the maternity hospital a lorry went out of control and smashed into their car.

She delivered her son in the wreckage but the ambulance men were unable to save the young parents, who were later buried together in the family vault.

The orphaned boy grew up in his grandfather's house, a solitary thoughtful child who wanted to be a doctor.

One day he said to his grandparents, 'Why do we never go into the library in the evening? It is a lovely room, with sunshine in the evening.'

His grandparents exchanged a swift glance. 'We just don't, not any more. You can, if you like,' said his grandfather.

His grandmother half-rose from the table as the child ran out into the passage, but the man gently restrained her.

The boy went into the library and sat there. He sat there in the summer sunlight until half-past eight and still nothing happened.

Then the owner of the house put his head round the door and said to his summer visitor who had come to look at the books,

'Are you coming in to dinner?'

3

Adoration of the name 'Treviles'. 'Reviles', Brid mused to herself, 'Treviles. From the Latin, vilus, vile. French, vil. Clearly the Treviles were an old Huguenot family who emigrated from Brittany immediately before the St Bartholomew Day's Massacre and settled in Cornwall. Très, the French word for "very".'

'Treviles,' supporting herself on her elbow, watching him sleep, 'a very vile fellow. A family closely associated with all sorts of vileness, named and unnamed, vileness worn as a badge of honour. The Vile Ones. Worshippers of Satan. Yoni soit qui mal y pense. Worshippers of the blood of women. Travellers. Gentlemen of the Moon. Treviles. One man among three. The man in the Moon. An old witch family fleeing church persecution and burnings and tortures. Fleeing to Albion, the land of the Goddess, and its noble Order of the Garter. Order of the Jam-Rag. Lady Salisbury, dancing, dropped a garter, a witch-cord: honi soit qui mal y pense, said Edward, evil to him who evil thinks, and founded the most noble Order of the Garter. Or she had the curse, dancing, and dropped her towel from between her legs: yoni soit qui mal y pense. Cunt to him who evil thinks. Ye shall honour that whence ye emerged.'

'No,' said Gregory suddenly at breakfast, the butter-knife poised, 'Treviles is the same word as travail, meaning to labour, and it derives from the Cornish word "trevas", meaning tillage, crop, produce, harbour. We Treviles are a family of harvesters, people employed at harvest.'

'You ploughed me,' replied Brid, though aghast at the co-incidence, 'will you harvest?'

It was Robyn's time of the month for books, not for men. She kept to her room, experiencing no jealousy, since it was not her time of the month for jealousy, and breakfasted by herself. The other two had not appeared when she got into her car to motor to the An Cuntellow Library at the Royal Cornish Institution in Truro. The day was fine, not as warm as August days often were in Petroc, not so muggy; the wind gusted small high clouds through a blue sky, and there was a slight bite in the air, a hint of Autumn on the way. 'The last gathering of wood-strawberries. Bullfinches and redbreasts eat the berries of the honeysuckles,' said Gilbert White of this day. It was the day the Virgin was taken up to heaven. Brid had been living with them through the summer, and the arrangement was working, since Gregory loved and was interested in both women all the time, and each woman was relieved of the necessity of loving and being interested in Gregory every day of the month, as in an ordinary marriage arrangement. Robyn had found a crystallisation of her individuality taking place. She had given her first lectures at Ruan Minor and attended Endenberg's seminars at Tintagel College, and she was deep into her vision of things as woman and scientist. On these two levels she met Gregory. Brid however was involved in artistic work. She now worked in clay, modelling, rather than carving in hard stone, and regarded this art work as an apprenticeship not to analysis in the formal sense, for she declared her intention of returning to practice, but to healing. In this she provided the complement to Gregory's work on re-introjecting images: he preferred to return the inner image to the person he was working with in conversation, or to himself by meditation or writing poetry; Brid loved to bring the images slowly to life in the clay. Robyn thought Gregory was calmer now than he had been during last autumn and up to the spring: he had found the image he needed to work with, it was 'to cross the river' or 'to stop the river' so that one might cross it and meet the people on the other side. It was distressing to Robyn that he spoke so much of Mamie, Robyn's mother, but she concealed her distaste of this dwelling on past things, deciding that Gregory was entitled to ransack his past. As for her, she was more interested in what she was going to accomplish, not what had passed. She thought that Gregory's present interests were natural; as Jung had said, it is normal for a man in the second half of life to wish to relate himself to his inevitable end, and to consider the fate of those who had gone before him. A refusal to face up to the fact of death was the root cause of all neurosis.

Once in the great circular reading-room (modelled, of course, after the B.M. and donated by an anonymous millionaire to An Cuntellow) she filled in her book-slips for the journals she wanted. She knew that she would have at least half an hour to wait — visually and organisationally An Cuntellow library resembled the B.M. She wandered over to the reference shelves and took down the volume T of the big dictionary. The pages opened and her eyes ran down the columns. 'Trestle, tret, treve, trews.' A treve, she read, was a roof-beam, and the term was usually reserved for a particularly stable construction of three beams cut from the same tree that was resistant to the stresses of storms, flaws and winds. It was important to lay these beams with the grain of the wood in certain directions. She flipped over a few pages. 'Traumatism, traumato, travail . . .' she was surprised to learn the derivation from old French 'travailler' meaning to torment — she had no idea the feeling was so strong — and as it went back it got stronger, back through the vulgar latin 'trepaliare' meaning 'torture', and 'trepalium' which meant torture-chamber, and, literally and originally, an instrument of torture made with three stakes. Her mind moved slowly back over her lifelong memories of Gregory. She found the Cornish dictionary, which told her that the prefix 'tre' meant a dwelling-place, and 'vyl' meant horror.

Thus through two languages, the name Treviles meant Horrorhouse. Gregory Horrorhouse.

She closed her eyes and saw beyond the lids a man let down from a gallery upon a sharpened stake, and the paling went up his back-passage and emerged from above his kidneys. His mouth was gagged so that his screams could not be heard.

His eyes were bulging from his head so much that you wondered if the eyelids could stretch enough to close completely. Blood trickled from the corners of these eyes. There were tears too, tears of water, tears of blood. The man's legs were tied to a cross-bar to keep them apart and a dark slime ran down the wood. His arms were tied to another crossbar that fitted into the wood that had already passed through his body, and this cross-bar held his arms above his head.

A notice nailed to the cross-bar above his head bore the legend DEATH TO THE MIDIANITE WITCHES. As she watched the caption changed as though some person had deftly fitted another slide into the projector: DEATH TO GREGORY TREVILES.

Slow dissolve to a woman in travail: the midwife slaps the woman's contorted face and cries, 'Push, push! Die if you must but push, push!' And the midwife reaches down to tie the cord, she bites it through and a little blood smears her face, she takes the baby in her butcher's hands, it is greeny-blue and as she picks it up it blushes red all over its skin that shines with grease. The midwife shoulders open the door into the next room and hurries with the baby to the scrubbed kitchen table where the doctor, very young, very sheepish-looking, is waiting with his scalpel. With a quick deft gesture, he pulls down the tiny foreskin. Almost the very first breath of the baby is an angry shriek. Close-up of the doctor's black bag, to the side of which is riveted a small brass plate on which is inscribed 'Dr C. Young'. Tracking shot out of the kitchen, out along a dismal hall, through the paint-peeling front door that swings to behind the camera, down the overgrown garden path out through the broken gate down the cliff path to show the house that stands high up and lonely on a granite cliff. Pan along cliff scenery and close up on a lettered finger-board reading 'Treviles' and fade. Robyn felt a touch on her shoulder. She opened her eyes quickly. The attendant stood at her elbow offering her the bound volumes of J. Psychosom. Med.

That afternoon, Brid took a pair of shoes that did not need mending to the Cornish cobbler on the hill. She knew that he was a Cornish speaker, a Nationalist taking lessons from an older man. While they were examining the pair of shoes together, she said casually, 'Does the name "Treviles" have a meaning in Cornish?' 'Yes,' said the shoemaker sourly, 'it means "the house on the old cliff".'

4

The perfume of his body, thinks Brid. I notice it wherever he has been. I like to be where he is for it, I love sitting in the chairs he has used, I love using his towels. I converse with his perfume for hours without speaking. He leaves it, this pear-must odour, in the wings of his armchair. I am dozing. I am in a boat rocking along a stream of firelight passing through orchards that blaze with pears of solid light so that I have to close my eyes made only of water and transparent gristle and sleep in the light that is too strong for them.

You have broken my heart, thinks Treviles, like a great funerary slab, and out of the chasm grow new plants, new flowers. My life is cracked across between Robyn and Brid and between you both at nights gestures the red-haired Mamie-ghost I do not believe in. As a young man, I had an ardent wafer-heart, like a Host. Then it became a pocket-mirror heart. When I went into practice this heart was a thin brass plate, inscribed with my name and my qualifications, and the heart was fastened with heart-screws to a door, which led to my consulting-room. If I was happy, if Mamie was happy, it was easy for us to enter this door. As time passed it became more elegant, and the key grew stiffer in the lock. At first it was a Finchley door, later it became a St John's Wood door. Then there were two doors, a town door and a country door. Then there was only a country door. Then there was a tomb. Then the tomb split.

This armchair smells of the dog. There are long red hairs on the white cushion. This armchair smells of horses. Even in winter there is an inch of grass on her grave. One hundred horses graze in this pasture. From beyond the grave, she pushes up green grass. Mamie was planted there three hundred years ago. An inch of grass grows there every day, winter and summer: in rain, two inches burgeons. Therefore, at a conservative estimate, she has grown from beyond death, one mile, one thousand two hundred and eighty-one yards and two feet of grass, if you neglected the double growth on rainy days.

As a horse eats roughly X cubic miles of grass in a year, and foals twice, and the herd grows exponentially at the rate of XYZ, she has nourished approximately X hundred horses, or XY tons of flesh, bones and sinews reborn from the earth. She is the Nurse of the Horses. Not far from her grave is the ancient well of Ruan Minor which, tradition has it, springs from her wedding-ring, even though she is ash and the flame that runs everywhere, as Jonathan is. In the thin black-and-white world of the photograph, Jonathan stands beside Gregory Treviles, assisting his big brother in his laboratory, anxiously clutching a hot test-tube in a wooden clothes-peg. Gregory pours some clear fluid into a tall burette. Gregory is a precocious, non-erotic, neat-coiffed, shut-faced prig of a clever schoolboy. Jon is standing amazed, a wide-eyed chubby-faced child in the ghostly photo-floods, astonished at his brother's vivid practices, anxious to please, but with his long straight nose and his lips parted, wide-eyed with a ghost-look. Treviles's terrors began again, turning his face to that face, that of a sturdy infant out of his depth, and slowly Treviles is turning into that dead person. Again he made a great effort to recall the time of the picture. Was he really that priggish, straight-backed boy, standing beside row upon row of bottles of specimens and chemicals? Hitler's war was not so far off, and Gregory thought that the small boy with the test-tubes had grown to look like Hitler. Except when he looked like the ghost of a small unhappy boy.

It was Augustine the great founder of modern Christianity who hated and repressed his infancy: 'the weakness, not of the will of infant limbs is innocence'. The boy Treviles had been called unto him, and set in the midst of them for an example, and he said, Verily I say unto you, Except ye be converted, and become as little children, ye shall not enter into the kingdom of heaven. And young Gregory with the smarmed-down hair, pleased to be an example to such full-bearded men, stuck his nose in the air and poured clear liquid into a graduated burette. Augustine in his hatred of children, the bottle-nosed W. C. Fields of theology, expunged the earlier doctrine: that 'Jesus saw children who were being suckled'. The Apocrypha tells how He said to His disciples: those children who are joy at both ends, who ejaculate from one end, who are ejaculated into at the other, whose inner is the same as their outer, who are clothed in exterior cunt, whose above is as their below, whose male and female is as a single one, of these are the Kingdom of Heaven . . .

The child speaks to us; it is the womb speaking; I hold my portrait that is a womb-stone in my hand and it tells me that it is in the womb's forgetive rage that my Mamie lives, there is always a molecule of her somewhere in every womb, and the womb magnifies her force and form, and my cock goes in there, into any womb, to listen to and love her. In paintings of Augustine, his attributes are a heart, whole, broken, or transfixed — and a book. He is sometimes shown with a small boy at his feet.

He saw this child on the beach, and the child was trying to empty the sea into a hole in the sand, with a scallop shell. When Augustine told him that his efforts were in vain, the child replied that his task was no harder than Augustine's attempts to expound the Trinity.

5

He asked them both:

'What do you think about when you're making love?'

'Secret.'

'Often, just as you put it in, I'm on one of our walks together.'

'Where mostly?'

'Oh, the deer park, down Fentonluna Lane.'

'I sometimes find myself back at the Mill.'

'I've never been there.'

'Robyn has. But it's as if you were there too, Gregory.'

'I met Brid at the Mill.'

'I know.'

'It's not the exciting walks that come back.'

'What do you mean, exciting.'

'It's the calm ones. The ones when several realities all came together and said the same thing, solidly, that come back like this. The exciting ones are like a change-over, a transition, like changing trains at a station.'

'You mean the Terrors.'

Gabby jumped off the bed, retreating to the hearth-rug.

BRID:

A little girl in blue, in her right hand a riding-crop, in her left a little horse held by the reins; out of the window a flash of lightning.

As Brid said, turning, 'I like this painting . . .' there was a flash of lightning outside the window.

She smiled.

'I hope there's a postcard of this painting,' she said. 'If not will you photograph it for me, Gregory?'

At the desk in the hall, there was a postcard.

'Oh,' said Brid in disappointment, 'but where's the lightning-flash?'

She frowned at the lady attendant. Gregory looked away from the two women, embarrassed. Bridget was occasionally capable of making a scene.

'I'm sure I don't know where the lightning is,' protested the attendant.

'But look,' said Bridget tensely, 'in the picture upstairs, the picture of Miss Carstairs dressed for riding . . . well, somehow she got her horse indoors for the painter, and there's this big window over her right shoulder and a flash of lightning in blue twilight.'

The older woman shrugged.

'So maybe it's another picture.'

Brid took a deep savage breath.

'Well THIS does say on the back of the postcard Miss Carstairs Dressed For Riding so can I see the curator please?'

'He's not here today.'

'I'll see his assistant then. Or anybody.'

'I'm the only one here.'

Bridget turned on her heel. She cried out in a voice shrill with period:

'Gregory! Gregory!! Come back here!'

Dr Treviles returned from the garden, sheepishly.

'Gregory, this lady says this is the only picture of Miss Carstairs . . . no, she doesn't say that, she says she doesn't know why there's no lightning on the postcard.'

Gregory started to answer, but he was interrupted by a soft intelligent voice that spoke from behind them.

'I'm Miss Carstairs, can I help?'

They whirled round, Gregory with his red-grey beard, Brid with her hair dark and soft as shadow.

'Miss Carstairs?' they said, 'but . . . ?'

'The little girl in the picture was my grandmother,' the elderly lady told them with a smile.

'Of course,' sighed Brid, 'but can you tell me why there is no lightning in the postcard, Miss Carstairs?'

'Why of course, Dr Hare,' said Miss Carstairs, coming closer and taking Brid by the hand, 'it would startle the horse.'

Brid jumped and pulled her hand away.

'Gregory, let's go,' she said out of the corner of her mouth, edging towards the exit.

Gregory stared at Miss Carstairs with growing apprehension.

'If you think you're being funny, Miss Carstairs, let me tell you that my fiancée and I are not amused. We came here in good faith and enjoyed the pictures and the atmosphere and all we asked was . . .'

The elderly lady nodded.

'I quite understand, Dr Treviles.' It was Gregory's turn to start. 'I will look through the postcards and find you one with lightning on it. Here's one. Are you quite sure you want to take it?'

'Yes,' said Brid firmly.

'Thank you very much,' said Treviles, handing over his five pence.

'Please call again.' Miss Carstairs floated after them.

'What a funny lady.' They walked between the topiaries of the lawn.

'Look!' cried Brid, 'look at the little horse in the paddock over there. The gate's open, it's coming across to us. I wish I had a lump of sugar or an apple.'

'Offer it some grass.'

The strong soft lips and the breath that smelled sweet and warm, the large brown eyes inspected the couple, blew delicately through its nostrils, and then the little horse wandered away and melted into the shrubbery.

'Unusual to let it wander. Look, there it is, among the nettles.' Gregory pointed.

'If that thunder-cloud breaks, we'll be drenched,' said Brid, and at that instant rain smelling of trade winds began and the whole gardens smelled of the sweet breath of the little horse. Everywhere the earth breathed out the little horse's wholesomeness.

Suddenly a hot door opened and closed near them, leaving them breathless and tingling from head to foot.

'That was lightning,' said Brid unnecessarily.

'We'd better get out of these trees,' said Gregory, 'come on, back to the house.'

They ran back across the lawn, the thunder-ordnance deafening them.

In the hail, Miss Carstairs stood, as if waiting for them.

'Well,' laughed Brid, panting a little, and shaking out her raincoat, 'we've seen some real lightning and a real pony!' Now she was anxious to make up with Miss Carstairs, and she flashed her one of her most winning gipsy smiles.

The lady of the house frowned and gestured at the window, which was blazing with sun and blue sky. 'There are no horses kept in these grounds nowadays,' she said coldly, as she began to climb the stairs.

ROBYN: A gusty day walking along the coast, towards the trees. I have left the beach of sand, and I am walking along the concrete causeways, across the marshes. I am walking east, towards Pentac Point. The Point is thickly wooded. An inlet of the sea separates me from its bushy trees, which are in constant activity from the wind. Leaves swing among other leaves like green monkeys leaping from bough to bough. A single puff of wind shapes the passage of a monkey from this bough, and as it travels on, another bough takes the same shape, so that the wind in the leaves makes a monkey that swings from tree to tree. Then a great wind rises that fills the boughs with chattering green monkeys. And a greater wind fashions a tall green man who strides among the canopies of leaves as through green surf. He turns round in the foaming surf and rises dripping in green and as he travels on towards the sea he shows great mouths in his body which open and close with soughing. I watch him break out of the wood and walk over the seashore, and see the tall white squall retreating over the waves in its wet draperies towards Ireland.

I step off the causeway on to a small beach of pebbles and sand. I pick up a flinty pebble that interests me and I hold it in my freckled fist. The pebble is hypnoglyphic. I run my thumb over its two small bumps like buds and over its crevices. My fingers warm it as though I were the sun warming a hilly landscape, rubbing the night-damp away with my long fingers, over the old stone peaks, turfy greens and misty ponds, waking the households with the cock-crow, rolling away the clouds of the mountains and as I grow higher in the sky warming woods, man and beast — that's enough! The stone is hypnoglyphic, it is a trance-stone, its world will draw me into its heart. I fling the hypnotic flint away from me. It strikes a boulder and snaps in two pieces. The impact of it also chips the boulder.

In the half-light of the thundery weather, I see a glow in the chipped crater of the boulder. I do not believe what I see. I creep a little closer. It is a beam striking upwards from the chipped rock, cutting into the black cloud directly above. I move closer. A tight beam of light is pouring from the boulder at an angle of about eighty-five degrees into the cloud-barrier.

And the cloud is beginning to swirl and disperse around the ray. The sun strikes through the storm-clouds and the ray from the boulder is washed out by the yellow sunshine. Now it is almost invisible.

I take a page from my notebook and pass it across the invisible ray. The paper is instantly cut away in a thin line. A sliver of paper flutters to the ground.

There is no mistake. A laser-beam, thinner than a pencil-lead, is emerging from the broken skin of that rock. I take a few steps back. What of the hypnoglyph? I search gingerly among the small stones and sand. I take my reading-glasses out of my skirt-pocket and put them on. There! a little further than I would have expected towards the Point I notice a slight snaily sparkle on the ground. It is a furrow marked, about an inch in diameter, sparkling slightly like the mucus track that might be left by a very large snail.

I reach out to touch it, then have second thoughts. I use my pencil instead. The shine shears the top off the plastic biro. I stare wonderingly at it, and at the tip of the finger I was about to use.

At the foot of the shine, on my right, I see half of the shattered hypnoglyph, the broken yantra. It too has beamed a ray of coherent light of great power but this ray is directed on and into the ground, like the furrow of a bullet, splashed with silvery lead. The cutting of this ray into the small pebbles and sand-grains has released their laser-beams, fortunately of small power in producing no more than this snaily scintillation; otherwise I should have been pierced through and through with arrows of almost invisible light like a Saint Sebastian. Punctured, I should have fallen forwards on to the furrow to be slowly sawn in half by the little rays shifting under my weight, or totally dissolved as they worked through me, or left as a few impossible mutilated rags of Robyn if their power gave out before they had quite consumed me.

I decided I'd best leave the beach now. I noticed that the furrow at its other end became a tunnel, and I did not know how far the flint's beam penetrated into the earth, nor what fantastic compact boulder-beams, or the lasers of whole strata, it might be releasing now. I would ring up the physics department, or, better, ask my professor to do so, and he would organise the proper research teams. But now it was time for me to leave, choosing my footsteps very carefully.

Safe on the causeway, I looked down at the quiet beach. Here, I thought, the skins of the rocks are wearing thin, and the skins of the grains of sand. Matter is turning into light on this beach. The ecology was partly alluvial and partly littoral. The researchers would determine whether the impatience of light to be released from stone, from its many stony skins, was greater in the river, or in the sea. I suspected the river, for the marsh over which I had walked had a reputation for Wills o' the Wisp.

I believe that the products of the erosion of many kinds of stone had settled here, brought down out of the ancient mines of Cornwall by the river, light more solid than the stone, a rotting marsh of star, of interlacing beams producing what new moirés, what interlacing patterns, what new wave-fronts of creatures set the one against the other, what new animals and plants, what new intelligences and experiments of light on our earth?

Very stirring, Robyn. Let me tell you mine. He reached out and Gabby, the red setter, trotted obediently towards the bed, settled herself in a convenient position for caressments.

Treviles: Autumn again. Treviles walks through the long wet grass with its slightly brownish tinge. The leaves drift from the trees, a precipitation of crystals. There is the fruity, dungy cold smell of the air, a beard-smell. He inhales it with pleasure and it has a sudden and most unexpected flavour. He pauses and inhales again slowly, deliberately. It strikes down to his palate like alcohol. Aromatic, yes, the taste of dry sherry, with a meaty flavour, as though mixed with hot soup.

This is excellent!

Treviles steps over to the park bench and sits down, careless of the wet. He sits down and relaxes, for he believes he knows what is coming next, and he wishes to enjoy it to the full. Over the next hour, in leisurely succession, he enjoys the soup, the fine flaky turbot with a hock, an excellent tournedos mingled with sips of Beaune, ice-cold raspberries and champagne chilled to tranquillity. He sighs. Then, still on his park bench, he enjoys a cup of coffee, Bisquit, and a good cigar.

The naso-pharyngeal apparatus of the diner transmitting this pricey clairgustance now leaves the restaurant. Gregory snuffs up the less pleasant exhaust fumes of the street beyond the restaurant door.

Gregory looked up the hill just as a portly middle-aged man

turned into the lane leading to the High Street and started walking down towards his park bench. Treviles knew that this was his 'agent', to whom he was 'percipient'.

As the portly man, puffing a little, passed Gregory's bench, the eyes of the two locked together for a moment. Gregory smiled, but his communicator looked away, stumbled, muttered an obscenity and walked quickly on without a word. He was a clergyman, and wore a white god-collar. Gregory wanted to speak to him, he wanted to know whether his 'agent' had transferred all the taste of his meal to his 'percipient', rendering his own meal tasteless, or whether they shared, and by sharing enhanced, but before he could call out fierce stomach-cramps that brought tears to his eyes doubled him up on the bench. The ghostly meal had made him ravenously hungry.

The dog stirred and lifted its head. A chill comes through the open bedroom door.

MAMIE: It is a chilly afternoon out on the hills. There is a little snow in the wind. Gregory stands on the shore of Stithian's Reservoir. He wants to stop the water and meet the people on the other shore. He wears a red shirt and black trousers. He is not cold. The pent water stretches away under the cloudy Cornish sky and in its curious light looks like a thin sheet of smooth tin, or a membrane stretched like that of a drum.

Not a ripple disturbs its surface.

He is a Diana's forester, a gentleman of the shade, he is a Moon-Man, and he wears Her colours; his face is white for the waxing and waning, right face and left; his shirt is red for love and the shedding of blood and the full moon of harvest; his trousers are black for the death of the moon; his feet are bare, the curve of the left foot signifying the waning moon, the curve of the right the waxing of the moon. He wears no tie, the shirt is open so that the left collar-tab may signify waning and the right waxing. He is the man between the two. The vee of his open shirt is the female triangle with point down; were it buttoned to the neck the collar would make the male triangle with point upwards. The complete glyph makes the Star of David, or the Sri Yantra, with triangles interlacing, or the monogram of Amor Vincit, with his round face the O of Omnia crowning the A.

If the water chooses to drown him, there are no better colours to die in; these are said to guarantee immortality. As it is he wishes for a better outcome.

His toe touches the smooth grey water. He advances with his right foot. A ripple runs out from the touch like the vibration of a drum.

He taps again, a second ripple runs after the first towards the farther shore. The first wave touches the hummocky bank, and begins to return. It collides with the second wave, and a sudden moiré pattern spreads over the surface. The instant this pattern appears, two heads come over the hill opposite. Bridget and Robyn with the dog Gabriel begin to descend the slope towards the water. They wave and call to him, but he cannot hear what they say, so he steps forward on to the water on to the moiré pattern, which bears him up. The two women kneel and tap the water with the palms of their hands like people tapping a drum and their ripples run towards him crossing and intersecting until the sheet of water resembles the palm of a vast hand stretched out to hold him, but a palm in which the lines change and reassert themselves differently every moment, writing a new meaning, a new life.

He walks onwards over the water, which feels like a thin cold sheet stretched beneath his feet. In the soles he can feel a buzzing from the moirés and the larger ripples rock him so he has difficulty in keeping his balance. The water has the instability of a trampoline. He calls out to the women, with the small firm waves running under his feet, 'Not so much, girls! I'll lose my balance!' crying out and laughing loudly as the little ripples run under his feet.

He walks with arms outstretched for balance like a man on a tight-rope that hums in the air. He walks with little quick steps now, still laughing, feeling the firm surface beginning to run a little, to become a little tacky in places, like road tar melting on a hot day, shimmering.

The women call out to him from the shore, not very far away now, calling with their arms outstretched, smiling with such sweetness it is as if they are encouraging a child taking its first steps alone, helping it with their voices to keep its balance until it reaches their arms.

Treviles can feel the cool water lapping about his bare ankles and then with a quick dancer's step he reaches the shore and mounts the cool turf. There are tears of pleasure in Brid's eyes and he embraces her first, then Robyn, the dog capering around, the three companions and their animal laughing and embracing by the waters of the reservoir.

6

'And whom do these terrors serve?'

'The dead, I think.'

'You'll not bring that back. You said it would unmake you. We have met it enough times even in our peaceful lives without asking it in. We have seen enough messengers breaking into our love with their tidings.'

'The seal.'

'That was certainly one of them. But there were so many. You ignore your doctor's training. You ignore Jon's terrible death. Do you want to bring that back, bruised like a rotten apple, nid-nodding like an idiot?'

'The seal was awful!'

'It was unexpected. We didn't know it was there. Hand in hand we wandered along, prettily, exclaiming at the famous beach's even-sized pebbles. It was washed up near the larger boulders at the end, looking like one of them.'

'You looked at me with a smile that meant you would welcome anything. I saw that there was a deformity among the boulders. I knew that the humped macintosh shape was something very dead.'

'Its head lay back with a great gash in its throat. The head lay on the back and the throat was open like some gladiatorial cry.'

'Like a wet mattress wrapped in a black rubber sheet.'

'Dead it was alive. It was roaring silently.'

'You tried to slip past it.'

'The smell lay athwart the beach like a black sunbeam you could not see. Or like black water.'

The afternoon of love and walking had thrown us into a trance, like children of genius who would believe anything they were told. We did not expect to have to break our trance and deal with a dead thing.'

The seal lay to their right, the sea to their left. Its body was swollen, the skin tight and shiny. This skin had split in several places, and the subcutaneous tissues were also tight and shiny, like a rotten black macintosh that had split open to reveal a rotten brown macintosh that had split open to reveal torn brown oilskins. Gregory stepped forward into the smell: his head was filled with rank horsesweat and beating black banners of faintness as though an immense army were running down on him. He stepped back and the sensation ceased. These decays of the dead thing knew a swifter chemistry than he possessed; he acknowledged a kinship; the normal decays of Gregory's body, the gentle warmth, the slight ammonia, the calloused toe whose skin splits, her rank and odorous monthly pad whose smell choked him, but eagerly interested the dog. And just as this couple out of their love-trance inspected and exclaimed upon the still stones that were like jewels to their eyes, were they not in turn inspected by the enormous smell-ghost of the seal, burning sideways like a dark flame that was a legion, he picking his way kindly over pebbles, she swimming on the wind in her yellow coat?

Brid bent over her white birthday-cake.

The icing on the cake glistened, and so did the white sequins on her skirt.

Do you mind if I wait a minute before blowing out the candles? she asked. I like to see them lighting the table. The food looks neater, more

Heavenly? White food for the dead!

Brid frowned, bent again and puffed out the candles. In that same instant a breeze blew down the dark lane and ruffled the curtains. The trio stood in darkness.

Now the food is black, said Brid, with satisfaction.

We walk the cliff-path until we look down upon the village where we shall find the seal-sanctuary.

There are seals in a stained crater. A shallow swimming-pool of concrete for the Cornish seals. There were some scribbles of dark amber urine, some thick yellow trails. But we are lovers. Everything looks lovely to us. Hence the name 'lovers'.

'But something is wrong', said Gregory.

The seals are dying. Their eyes are yellow dishes containing a dark fluid. We loved the seals when we saw them in their better time and we love them still.

Gregory asked the seal-keeper:

'Why is there no water?'

Sadly, the man looked up at them and said:

'The seals are sick. They have viral jaundice. A rat brought it in. The rat's urine has got into the water.'

'Oh!' said Mamie, paling. She felt the whole rat-shape of her mouth, her throat outlined in living fire as she breathed this yellow air.

Gregory steered her up the steps and they looked sadly at the seals. Gregory turned.

'Will you catch it?' he asked their keeper, meaning, will I catch it, will she catch it?

The mouths were cat-pink and full of dogs'-teeth. They were neat-headed. They were yellow death. They stank of human fear.

The keeper blew out his cheeks and shook his head.

'Two of them have gone. Myself, I feel so low about it I can't tell. I don't much care what happens to me, I'm taking tablets in case, doctor's orders. These . . .' he gestured towards the unhappy animals '. . . are being injected tomorrow. Once they've turned yellow they're gone.'

Mamie swallowed in a dry throat and her head ached. The seals drag themselves across dry concrete, the pool is empty because they must not splash their water, it is dangerous, the virus enters the body through the skin, it destroys the red corpuscles and turns them yellow. The lovers, dead and shivering, remember those bodies last spring like beneficent shellfire with their crisp splashes, bullet-sleek, agile water made more agile by these water-gymnasts. The sunlight is yellow, and does not warm them as they leave through the wire gate. Is the fever of jaundice full of visions? Is this detached genetic code gone wild and mad that imposes the experience of jaundice on you just as your heredity is imposed on you in the act of generation, the passionate thoughts of dead people? If Gregory dies before me, wondered Mamie, will I remember him best in feverish dreams?

Gregory made the commemorative shrine with the photograph on the west side of the room in which he intended to hold the Dumb Supper. The picture of Mamie in her nurse's uniform, red cape, red hair, stands in its frame on a black cloth. Two vases flank the photograph, masses of fresh flowers, wild flowers picked from the river bank that afternoon. The long table, positioned so it is lying east-west, is spread with a freshly-laundered white tablecloth on which the square of black with the flowers and picture shows like a trapdoor. Gregory has eaten nothing all day. He lays Mamie a place in the east, opposite her picture, which to her ghost as it is forming itself will act as a simple mirror on a dressing-table. He himself sits in the south, facing another empty chair in the north. He keeps his eye averted from Mamie's empty chair at all times. Spoon, knife and fork, and wine-glasses for them both.

Lych-gate. Corpse-gate. Lecher-gate. Mamie and Gregory glide under the lych-gate, into Mawnan Smith churchyard. The lintel of the gate was supported by solid granite blocks and the inscription above in Cornish said 'It Is Good For Us To Draw Nigh Unto God'. The right-hand pillar was inset with a slot labelled 'for your parking', the left with another reading 'for the upkeep of the churchyard'. They had approached from the north, towards the coast. This was a mariner's church, and was still used as a seamark. The first graves they encountered were recent and prosperous. A few small, carefully-tended saplings bent in the breeze from the sea in labelled memorial beds. As they walked to the right, around the locked west door of the church, they found that a small stone patio had recently been built, and on it were several park benches of light new wood, also remembrances.

To the south they found many more graves crowded together, mostly very old, dating back to the first years of the eighteenth century. The church rose behind as solid as a cliff. But there was one very fresh grave there, piled with fleshy funeral flowers, voluptuous garlands, no more than a night old. Mamie stared at the grave without speaking.

The presence of the grave chilled Gregory with a sick image of the freshly-rotting body. He thought that if he took a lamp underground, the colours of death would be as bright as these flowers above, and the odours of death would glare and sicken me and I would close my living nostrils against them, as I close my eyes against the sun, this black sun of odour. Yet they are only waxes and oils, body-odour, blood, perspiration, smelly dolls of wax rendered gigantic by death. Not friendly and dry and quite forgotten like those old graves, grinning nicely, clean straight bones, a little ragged vellum of skin, some dusty red hair, no more offensive than spider-webs. Instead, while the universe of the very small works inside them, the little bright death-gods chewing away, a stiff wax doll, jerking, belly swelling up with marsh-gas, monstrously daubed and cloaked with the ten thousand colours of the full smell-chord of a city's thousand neglected shit-houses.

Mamie had dropped to one knee by the grave. She was reading the paper labels attached to the wreaths. She looked up at Gregory wonderingly, and said 'Look at this Gregory . . .' but Gregory averted his eyes. He did not want to know the name of the dead person.

He moved as quietly over the carpet as he could, and kept his eyes averted from the chair meant for Mamie's ghost. Then he served the white food from the sideboard, walking always with his face averted from the chair. A spoonful of clear soup, an inch square of fish and potato, in a separate dish, a thimble's helping of creamy trifle. Every plate and dish was also white and he poured a few drops of a white wine in each glass. Then he removed the white veil from the portrait and sat down at his place. As the clock on the mantelpiece began to strike midnight, he started to eat. The clink of his fork on the plate was loud in the room, was there an echo of this small noise, as though another person also fed? The only light in the room came from the candles on either side of Mamie's photograph, and the pure scent of her wild flowers reached out on the air to him. The candles wavered as he ate his dumb supper with his eyes downcast and the chair opposite him filled with strange shadows, but always he kept his eyes averted from the chair to his right.

When he had finished his supper, which in his fasting state, burned colours of taste on his tongue, he paused again, with head bent, as if praying. Then he pushed back his chair and still with eyes turned from the east, walked the few paces towards the picture. Reaching out, he extinguished the candles neatly, with finger and thumb, whispering Mamie's name as he did so. Her two names.

Then he lifted his eyes to her chair.

The door opened slowly, blinding him. In its outline he saw the figure of a woman glide swiftly into the room. There was a click and the overhead lights blazed out. Robyn stood in bare feet with her red hair loose. He realised that she was now the same age as her mother was when she died.

7

Robyn had left for bed after kissing him when she understood what he had been trying to do. Dr Treviles sat at the long table in his place in the full glare of the overhead lights, his head in his hands, dry-eyed, no feeling in him. It was as though he had come to the end of a long road that something in him, which had died as the big lights in the overhead chandelier came on, had made interesting, every inch of it. This 'something' was his jewel, his imagination, 'mon bijou, mon âme' his invention which he allowed to surround him, toys diverting him at every moment. It was dead, this thing in him, and the dead were dead also, and did not come back, except in their children. What kind of survival was that, without memory! Nature had no memory.

He frowned, and felt something turn against itself on his face, like a cloth or a veil, like a coating of wax. Something drifted past his eyes and he looked down at his hands. There, resting on his open palm, was a waxy replica of his own expression.

He wanted to fix it back on his face, but just as he shifted it back into position he felt a new looseness on his skin and the second mask came loose.

He got up from the table and walked about the room. Mask upon mask drifted from his face. The room is adrift with them, like snowflakes or pale feathers. He picks one up, it is translucent and shows every detail, down to the small transparent windows that have sloughed from the surface of the open eye. As he realises this, his eyes blur and another mask falls from his face.

He hurries out into the hall to see what expression, what face to face himself is left, but the masks are coming so rapidly now that he cannot glimpse his true face in the blur of them as they fall off. He opens the door and steps out into Fentonluna Lane. The stiff wind that is blowing pulls the masks away from his skull, layer upon layer, mask upon mask of terror blowing away on the wind like smoke from a bonfire. He stands there as they dislodge more slowly now, bending around in the breeze as if to look at him, or to show themselves to him before they blow away on the seaward wind. He sees himself at Endenberg's conference, inquisitive, the mask has a ghostly finger to its nose to make it look wise, he sees himself as he spoke first to Brid, and he sees his lover's face as he knows he looked when he first slept with her; he sees himself in the train, determined, mad; he watches himself at the dumb-feast, and two tears have left their impression on the wax, like candle-tears. He sees himself as small Hitler, with the sad face of his brother, bruised and broken, over his shoulder. All his terrors pass by him in visions like masks as he stands there with the fresh Cornish wind on his face. Finally, he has seen all that is shown him, the masks have stopped coming. He turns round and enters the house. The hall is littered with no masks. He picks up the dishes of the dumb supper and takes them into the kitchen and puts them in the sink. His own face greets him in the mirror. He believes he will allow God to choose his face for him.

THE END OF THE TERRORS OF DR TREVILES

Appendix

ROBYN'S CANDLE POEMS

THE DEFEAT OF THE TROLLS

for Gregory

Only one candle unmasks
the room
and my reconnoitres of the room
are dependent on the candle flame

The pastoral map
on the wall absorbs the land-locked
light
Megalithic ghosts dart
across the doorway, wedging into the light

There was danger today
heaving upwards with the redolence of gun-barrels
and horse-sweat
Tonight I draft my poems in red ink
No other colour can describe
the day's forfeits,
decipher the stale stories of the invaders

My book calls 'dittany' the candle plant
I love candle-light
Candles cause nights and dark mornings
to become deckled,
with edges uncut,
no doors closed

Fear fetched down from the old places
exhausted me today,
glowering through the outbursts of love
When I woke, the day smelt like the stage
of an ancient theatre

In the day, there were veiled colours
tamping the waters

There was a wintry tree full of brown birds
with beaks the colour of sawdust

There was a sea composed of grey feathers
I saw these mitigating things
I crunched the beauties up

But the apparel I wore
was wrinkled by my bad thoughts,
the clothes curdled on my flesh,
the fabrics were replete with cold,
patches of iron were nailed to my skirt

All day, bitter clowns spoke through my mouth

Until this evening
when we laid aside our old clothes,
our frightened thoughts,
and embraced

and bridges rippled snakily between us
in the infallible dance of lovers,
the webby consummation,
all the fragments frolicking together

Rising in the darkness,
we are the mended ruffians
Our smiles are no longer retarded

In your room, you read the magical book
In the next room, I light this candle,
zodiacing the room with cornish colours,
to celebrate the vanquishing
of the murky rabble,
the trolls who tried to catch our breath

MAN WALKING ON ROOF

My candle is red and round as a tomato
It is a gift-shop candle, a tourist toy
It is not the old white candle of the lovers,
blown out for secrecy,
it is not the unfathomable candle
that answers the insinuations of the priest

It is not the apprehensive candle
of the confined woman regretting her marriage,
it is not the candle
that was once the marrowbone of beggarly winters

No, this candle is a toy, a novelty

I light the candle
The predatory flame begins eating at once
A fall of red wax winds down into the saucer
The candle ball tilts
I hear the fuse spit, the tiny roar
of a heraldic lion

From an upstair window I look out
across the blue roofs of the town
Light rain falls, smelling of shabby clothes
As I watch, a man appears, walking on a roof
He moves quietly, uncertainly
Perhaps he is walking in his spoony afternoon sleep
I watch as he approaches the edge
He turns, stoops, he mends the wind-damaged chimney
with vexed gestures,
sensing that his roof-solitude has been broken

The candle,
smaller than the apple I am about to eat,
stands back from the lights and darks of my page

There is a strangeness
about this ordinary candle
that can summon a man to the rooftops
The candle says that my long oblique path
through winter, moon-dark, candle-lit,
is leading me to where
all but the brightest stars are quenched

And I must learn the words of welcome
to open the doors of that prismatic house
I glimpse through this opaque window

TRAVELLING

Across blue fields to find Satan
White stars above me, roots of fire
I want to unlock the keys of the piano

On volcanic islands I hear the passage
of clumsy adults without wings
I am one of them

Rain falls, many delicate colours
appear in the distance
Satan throws winter across his shoulder

I climb the hodden-gray hills
From the harbour I hear the hoarse
tender warning of the foghorn

There are no dinosaurs drinking
at the river's edge
I stoop, I throw a handful of red earth
into the river
There is no time to write a treatise
on this subject

I looked for Satan in the polar lands
My breath stood solid in the air
Cold seized me by the throat, made me helpless
But I did not find Satan,
could not touch his fiery rank flesh

I laboured in a summer garden
Women and children dressed in garish red garments
watched me

In their hands, they held bunches
of flowers, feathers and branches
Four women came towards me,

they related reminiscences to me until dusk,
and the children sat on the lawn, watching

I stand at the door of the granary
I snuff up the odours of harvest
Behind me, Satan is looking for his women
His jaw opens, extends into a beak
I walk to the edge of a steep place
I am looking down into the second sign of the zodiac
Darkness grows up in black clusters around me

But I step back from that edge
I enter a different darkness, it is the dark of the barn,
the sweet stench of the grain

CANDLE ON A RAINY MORNING

Raindark, a morning of thin magic
My room is lost beneath the shadows
of the family tree,
dilemmas of leaf, branches budding with memories
How can I pilgrimage beneath this blind and deaf tree
with its wrinkles of riches?

My room is the family forest
The skins of the window-pane shudder
Their veiled aunts smile, chill and tardy
I can't sing or write my letters
The leaves are whispering like mother and father
My brother's laughter warns me from the topmost branches

What danger? I ask
What danger?
He laughs and points down at me
I see the red feathers sprouting from my breast

I stand by the window
The flame of the candle is thoughtful,
a poor relation
The trees do not shed leaves but family photographs
The smiles litter the floor
Pressed flowers fall from the pages of my notebook

These dry handfuls of summer have the pallor of unwound clocks
It is noon and I am feverish, thinking
of the strangers from whom I inherit the family forest
Last night I dreamt of holy and royal infants
Now the rain falls yellow as yesterday

Again the trees are part of the ugly wallpaper
The sky lightens, makes my candle redundant,
leaves me watching the finger of flame embark
upon the sunlight, perplexed, shut up in childhood

THE EPIPHANY CHARM

Moons are worn away by darkness,
by the timbrels of stars,
eaten away by the eyes of women
Moons move and I move fretting
through the apprehensions of winter
Since the first day of this new year
I have been trapped in my talon-coloured room

For five days my hands
have been the instruments of germ-warfare
Each day has been spoilt by the anniversaries of conception
and I have walked, crookbacked,
my thoughts like time-fuses of private information
The malignity of my twilights
has been breaking all the world's mirrors

I have felt my makeshift bones twist,
gnarl in their growing:
I was afraid, I thought the year would rush past me,
go on to brilliancies and rewards without me,
perform the championships without me,
leaving me scoured of sleep
and tasting only the antiquities of ice:
I was scared of the accusers in their angry orbits,
saying to me, no, you can't, you can't . . .

I have come to the sixth of the new year's mornings
I thought it would contain as many complaints
as its five foreshadowers
but instead I have found the midwinter mandala
I have opened the books and entered their nimble worlds
I have met the penitents and the whores
They have spoken secrets to me and pointed out the footpath
that will lead me to a fruitful contact with my enemy

Now the names of things, *flower, candle, cloud:*
are part of my life again, and not dead words,
not the pestilential plumage of the lost year
Look, my hands are holding the messages, I unfold
my new skin, I am no longer the woman
with stiff hooked smiles, I am the woman drifting
calmly to the rhythm of the land and its waters

On my bookshelf, the hyacinth leans towards the light
I pin a brooch to my blouse, a deer,
the creature of Coventina,
another of the moon's concealed creatures

I turn the pages of my diary
Christ tweaks and twitches my skin with his feasts
But I shake my head, he is the wrong one,
he is the god of murderers

Only journeys through the passages of the moon
heal my telltale disease
Only the dreams I unravel, the coils of their rainbow rope,
give me back my own body, moon-resurrected,
rising from the sequence of dark awkward rooms

HER TIME OF THE MONTH

He is net and noose, spider and octopus,
The rooms are adrift,
There is a melting vat of wet butterfly wax,
I am a stripped wire, spitting.

My insulation's off, my father,
My heart, my father, my nether heart,
A pennywhistle sealed in a gauze cage plays,
Water is my hinger.

A heap of manure and squealing white wands,
I turn through the whelping-box

I turn through the mummy's tooth

I turn through the cream souring in thunder

I swine through the rain forest

I somersault through the bull's cut lip

I arrive again on the cool moon-plain
By the white tower
Under the full earth
The tower picks up its skirts

It runs after me shouting
Mother Pater, Mother Pater,
Blushing thunderously
Braying from its musketry-loops

I want to turn through the clock face
But the clock strikes in his voice:
You are late! You are nearly a week late!

My akimbo womb takes up a new stance, because I'm not late.
He should have spoken quietly until I returned.
I go back under the ermine skirt-fall.

I hasten backwards through all my buttonholes,

The front buttonhole and the back buttonhole
The salt buttonholes and the waxy buttonholes
The sooty buttonholes and the ivory one

Now a seamless wax person drifts to the floor softly.
He spoke too loudly.
He spoke too early.
He will find a left-handed hole.
He has something for me he will put into that wax person.

THE CANDLEMAS HOUR

Many-coloured, the books
are breeding on the shelves
behind my back,
spawning the children of Candlemas

Someone has squashed a spider in the book of fairy-tales
She wasn't there last week
Someone put a goose feather between the torn pages
of the bible
Lucifer ploughs the fields, he whispers, 'salt . . .'
He has no shadow among the weeds

Patiently, I replace both books
Let the spider and the feather remain
Let them make their own decisions
Out of the reach of my eye, the book titles
grapple with each other and with Adam's first wife
Let the books ambush me, without their tricks
I cannot name my calamities

I have an hour to myself
I am listening, my skull trembles, I am waiting
for the deductions of the rainy morning,
I canter over the white doorsteps

I light the daytime candle
How many days are left to me
before the obese angels step into my room,
rustling leafy wings, holy at last,
golden ribbons in their many-coloured hair?
Books chatter excitedly behind me

I listen with my thumbs and big toes
The books are saying, eight days, eight days
There are eight days until Candlemas,

until you wear the scarf of radioactive legend,
until the old year has been eaten up
by the acrobats of the moon

Candlemas will reveal my next darkness,
a direction leading me to the dark,
a cellar of ebony butterflies, a cupboard
of black lace mittens

I nod, start walking, running
towards that long story of darkness
It will take me exactly one year
to reach that darkness,
one year to see its leafy shape, its ravines of snow,
its forests of lava

I will try to understand a small part of it
and cry aloud as I pass through it, striking
the darkness lightly with the palms of my hands

It may not be a black darkness
Last year it was a black darkness of mirrors,
goring my flesh with poverties and blindness

This year I stood back from the darkness,
I was not ready to look at it again, so soon
But next year I think it will be a darkness
of thin green fields,
or the darkness of red berries in a straw basket
Or it may be made of cold interesting smoke
and I also will be the darkness that is not dark

Out of each year's darkness, a gift comes
Even the darkness I did not look into
has given me many-coloured candles,
the beauties of blood, given me real flowers
for the first time
It has cleansed my wounds

and I have recorded the name of this year,
it is the Year of the Dew, that showed me all the moons

In eight days time, at Candlemas,
the earth's year begins, my year begins
It may be a year made from a garden
in which moves the dreaminess of snails,
or a year made from one single morning of maps
Even the shadow of a ratcatcher
may be the signpost I cannot avoid obeying,
do not wish to evade

Whatever direction it is,
the steep slope of gravel, the muddy valley,
the desert, the waterfall, the forest,
the months threaded with sea-birds
or marred by unkind letters: whatever leads
me to the dark residence beneath the smoke-dried stars,
I am ready for the Candlemas road,
I can walk down there into the dark, the plurals of light

I no longer need to wear the redhot robe,
the shoes made of sullen knives

I ride on the sledge of my blood

A TWELVEMONTH

In the month called Moth
I am the arachnoid bride
opulent among my webs

In the month called Smoke
the ice-birds do not let me forget
the chilliness of my candle

In the month called Glimmer
I strike the skeleton with my bare hand
and she is a delicate sorrow-sight
of coiling colours

In the month called Leaf
I go into the forests every third day
fishing for birds with my treacly nets

In the month called Axe
I wear red dresses
a compass round my throat on a silver chain
serves for my necklace

In the month called Page
I read books which the little liveried boys bring me
the books tell me stories about Neptune

In the month called Trapeze
I thumb a lift on the motorway
the man who rapes me gives me
the message I need, a perfect mystery

In the month called Feather
I walk warily in the fields of tinkling grass
the thin silk of my gown
is the husbandry of this land

In the month called Torch
the sharks are kissed by the sun
I postpone all my appointments

In the month called Birth
the blasphemer lights the red candle
plethora of wax gorges us

In the month called Root
I shiver with cold
the mordant rooms deepen with snow-light

In the month called Velvet
I iron my shadow hair-ribbons
my companion watches me, smiling
his antlers gleam in the fire-light

Peter Redgrove   Penelope Shuttle

The End Of Our Book

www.ingramcontent.com/pod-product-compliance
Lightning Source LLC
LaVergne TN
LVHW090950080826
845145LV00003B/962

* 9 7 8 1 9 0 5 0 2 4 0 9 4 *